COMFORT CROSSING HOLIDAY COLLECTION

KAY CORRELL

ROSE QUARTZ PRESS

Published by Rose Quartz Press

r101818110119

KAY'S BOOKS

Find more information on all my books at *kaycorrell.com*

COMFORT CROSSING ~ THE SERIES

The Shop on Main - Book One
The Memory Box - Book Two
The Christmas Cottage - A Holiday Novella (Book 2.5)
The Letter - Book Three
The Christmas Scarf - A Holiday Novella (Book 3.5)
The Magnolia Cafe - Book Four
The Unexpected Wedding - Book Five

The Wedding in the Grove - (a crossover short

story between series - with Josephine and Paul from The Letter.)

LIGHTHOUSE POINT ~ THE SERIES

Wish Upon a Shell - Book One
Wedding on the Beach - Book Two
Love at the Lighthouse - Book Three
Cottage near the Point - Book Four
Return to the Island - Book Five
Bungalow by the Bay - Book Six

SWEET RIVER ~ THE SERIES

A Dream to Believe in - Book One
A Memory to Cherish - Book Two
A Song to Remember - Book Three
A Time to Forgive - Book Four
A Summer of Secrets - Book Five
A Moment in the Moonlight - Book Six

INDIGO BAY ~ A multi-author sweet romance series

Sweet Days by the Bay - Kay's Complete Collection of stories in the Indigo Bay series

Or by them separately:

Sweet Sunrise - Book Three

Sweet Holiday Memories - A short holiday story
Sweet Starlight - Book Nine

Sign up for my newsletter at my website *kaycorrell.com* to make sure you don't miss any new releases or sales.

HOLIDAY COLLECTION

A set of two holiday books in the Comfort Crossing Series. (Books 2.5 & 3.5) See the whole series at my website:

https://kaycorrell.com/comfort-crossing-series

THE CHRISTMAS COTTAGE

A story of love, moving on, and a dog named Louie

Veterinarian Holly Thompson accepts a temporary position in Comfort Crossing in an effort to escape all things Christmas. What she finds is a small town that embraces all things Christmas and a handsome neighbor with a small son who both capture her heart. Add to that their adorable pup, and she knows the holidays are not going to be what she planned. At all.

Steve Bergeron is quite content being a single father. He's not willing to risk his heart — or his son's — on another woman who is sure to leave them. It's quite clear Holly will be gone by the new year. But he finds himself willing to do anything to chase away the sadness that lurks in the depths of Holly's eyes. This isn't part of his carefully laid out plans. At all.

When an accident on Christmas Eve forces them both to question their choices, can the magic of the season warm their hearts and bring love and joy back into their lives?

THE CHRISTMAS SCARF

Sometimes, Christmas wishes bring their own special magic...

Missy Sherwood has always wished for one thing, to be a country singer. After trying to make it for years in Nashville, she returns to her hometown of Comfort Crossing, Mississippi, feeling like a misfit and a failure. But there's no use in telling anyone the truth just yet—she's here for longer than the holidays, she's home for good. Right?

Dylan Rivers is glad to see his old friend return to town, not only to help him with the children's Christmas pageant, but because her homecoming sparks long-forgotten but never acted upon feelings. But there is no use in acting on those feelings, she's soon to head back to her fabulous career in Nashville. Right?

Then a stranger comes to town and has Missy re-examining her dreams. She gets one final chance at stardom, and her life-long wish is within her grasp. Is there really magic in the stranger's scarf, or is it in the power of knowing her heart's true wish?

COMFORT CROSSING ~ A NOVELLA

The Christmas Cottage

KAY CORRELL

Published by Rose Quartz Press

062917

ISBN: 978-0-9904822-4-6

This book is dedicated to all the believers in the magic of Christmas.

CHAPTER 1

Dear Reader,

If you're like me and like to read a series in order, The Shop on Main - Book One in the series, is available for FREE at this time. But all the books in the series can be read as stand-alone stories. Happy reading!

~ Kay

Holly pulled the car over to the side of the road. She flicked on the light on the ceiling of her beat up but serviceable sedan. It had done her well on the long drive. Good thing she'd written out the directions to Comfort Crossing in the middle of nowhere Mississippi because she'd lost her cell signal twenty minutes ago. Her map app on her phone was doing her no good. She snatched up the directions she'd hastily written on a scrap of paper. Maybe too hastily. She wasn't sure if this was where she was supposed to turn, or if she needed to go to the next intersection. After twisting the paper back and forth, as if that was going to make any difference, she decided it did say to turn left here.

Probably.

She pulled the car back onto the blacktop road and decisively made a left turn. This was the right way. Left way. Left was the right way. Well, she knew what she was talking about even if her brain was bouncing around trying to trick her.

What had seemed like such a good idea last week began to pale a bit as the day had worn on. She knew she was headed to a small town somewhere not far from the coast of Mississippi, but she hadn't realized just how far Comfort Crossing was from any real town. Though, she doubted the residents would like it if she said Comfort Crossing wasn't a real town. She'd keep that thought to herself when she began her work at Comfort Crossing Animal Clinic. Two weeks of work away from her home, family, and friends. Just what she craved this holiday. Long hours, lots of work, and just pop on over to the new year. Snap, just-like-that, the holidays would be over and life could get back to normal. Please.

Her headlights sliced through the darkness until she could see a glow coming from a town in the distance. Hoping the lights meant she'd found her destination, she drove on. She flicked on the radio and twisted the knob to see if she could get a signal. After a bit of static, the clear tones of a country singer belting out Jingle Bells poured into the vehicle.

Not a chance.

She quickly twisted the knob again only to be greeted with the melodious sound of Silent Night. The next station blared out Deck the Halls. Great. She stabbed at the off button. Didn't any station play normal music in December?

She pulled into town, thankful to see a sign declaring she'd found Comfort Crossing, and made a left on Main Street. The street was decorated with lights strung across it from sidewalk to sidewalk and bright red bows tied on each lamppost. The front of the stores were all decorated with holiday festivity, with snow etched snowflakes painted on the windows and Christmas displays beckoning customers to come in and finish off their holiday shopping. It looked like a vintage Christmas card for Pete's sake.

She gritted her teeth, ignored the decorations and continued down Main Street, looking for Chalk Road. There it was. She pulled under a street lamp and glanced at the directions one more time. Take Chalk Road about two miles. The cottage she was staying in was on the left. A red mailbox. That should be easy.

Four miles later she turned the car back around. She drove more slowly this time and spotted the red mailbox, cleverly almost hidden in a bush. Not such a great marker after all. She pulled into the gravel driveway and followed its curves up to a pretty white cottage.

Then she saw the twinkling white Christmas lights strung on the bushes lining the front porch. A wreath hung on the door. Red-ribboned bows hung from the porch railings. It was Christmas at this cottage, that was for sure.

Her worst nightmare.

Exactly what she did not want.

How could she have known escaping Christmas by hiding out in a small town and waiting for the holiday to blow past her would put her right smack into its midst? A place she did not want to be.

She pulled her suitcase out of her car and crossed over to the come-rest-a-spell front porch. Red Adirondack chairs and a swing were nestled at one end of the porch. Light poured through the big picture window. She could see into the cottage to a tidy family room with a fireplace against the far wall. She didn't realize it would get cold enough here in Mississippi in the winter for a fire.

Holly picked up the flower pot beside the door, and just like the instructions had said, there was the key. She opened the front door and crossed into the cheerful warmth of the cottage.

Holly unpacked her suitcase and settled in. Someone had left her coffee, milk, orange juice, a sandwich, and a delicious looking cinnamon roll. She guessed when Comfort Crossing needed a temporary veterinarian, they went all out to make you feel at home.

Her partners at the vet clinic in Kansas had known how hard this Christmas would be for her. When Lynn, not only her best friend but another vet at the clinic, had seen the ad for this temporary position she'd suggested that maybe Holly should take it. Holly had made no attempt to hide the fact that she wasn't having Christmas this year.

She was not decorating.

She wasn't going home to visit her parents.

She'd refused Lynn's invitation to have Christmas with her and her family.

Lynn, always looking out for her, had said spending the holidays in a place Holly had never been, without all the haunting memories, might be the best thing for her. It hadn't taken much to convince her that Lynn was right.

Lynn sure had been right about one thing. The stress and gloom that had been hanging over her all month had lifted as she drove down to Mississippi. She'd listened to an audiobook on the drive. When was the last time she'd listened to or read a book? It had been so long. She'd just tried to keep busy. Very busy. Always doing something, chasing away the memories. But as she'd driven down the highway, she'd felt herself relax for the first time in she didn't know how long.

Well, until she'd pulled into Christmas Town and then onto The Christmas Cottage. She wondered if she could just unplug those Christmas lights. That was a thought. Of course the Animal Clinic was on Main Street with its frighteningly over-decorated storefronts. She'd just ignore them on her way to and from work.

A dog barked outside the cottage and she stopped for a moment, frozen in time. No. Just a hint of a memory that she pushed firmly to the side before it could develop fully.

Then she heard the barking again. This time she knew it was real barking. Right outside.

"Louie! Come back here."

A voice called outside the cottage. Holly opened the door and was greeted by the most gorgeous Australian shepherd she'd ever seen. He jumped up on her in greeting, almost making her tumble back inside. She caught herself on the door frame. "Down, boy." The dog obediently sat at her feet. She noticed he had a full tail instead of the docked tail of most Aussies. It thumped against the porch flooring.

"Louie, Dad's going to kill me. Come back."

Holly heard a voice from around the corner. Just then a boy came barreling around the house and up to the porch.

"Louie." The boy took a big gulp of air. "Bad dog." The boy paused a moment to bend over and catch his breath. The dog got up and licked the boy's face.

"I'm sorry, lady. I'm supposed to train him not

to jump up on people. Or run away. He's supposed to come when I call. Which he usually does, but he saw a squirrel and ran off." His explanation came out in a rush of words.

"It's fine." It almost was. "His name is Louie?"

"Yep. Louie, sit."

The dog immediately sat.

"Nice." She was impressed.

"He's really good when he wants to be." The porch light gleamed off the boy's brown curly hair. His jeans had a rip in the knee. His baseball cap was slipping off the side of his head with locks of curly hair poking out wildly in all directions.

"Louie, down." Louie plopped down on the front porch. "See, he has lots of tricks."

"So your dog is Louie, what's your name?"

"I'm Josh. I live next door. Dad takes care of this house. It was my aunt's house. She moved away for work. We sometimes rent it out."

"Nice to meet you, Josh. I'm Holly."

"Nice to meet you. My dad won't let me call you Holly. I can call you Miss Holly though." The boy tugged at his baseball cap righting it back on his head, tilted back at a jaunty angle.

"Miss Holly it is then."

"Joshua." A deep voice called from the side yard.

"Over here, Dad."

A tall man came striding around the corner of the house and stopped short. "I'm sorry. Didn't know you were here yet. Hope Josh hasn't been bothering you."

"Not at all. Just getting to meet him and Louie."

The man sighed, walked over to Louie, bent down, and ruffled the fur on his head. "You're such a bad dog, Louie." His voice held warmth and affection and Louie's tail thumped against the boards on the porch.

"I'm Steve Bergeron. Live next door."

"I told her we watch the house for Aunt Lucy and rent it out sometimes," Josh explained.

"Lucy, my sister. Doesn't live here anymore but doesn't want to sell the house." Steve smiled at her.

"Nice to meet you, Steve. I'm Holly Thompson, but you know that since I recognize your name from our emails about the rental."

Steve nodded. "Doc Benson usually arranges for his temporary vets to stay here, not that he takes time off very often." The tall man lounged against a beam supporting the front porch. Louie sat obediently at his feet, his tail swishing back and forth.

"I start tomorrow. He's going to show me the ropes, then hopefully I can hold down the fort for his vacation."

"He was lucky to find you. I was beginning to think he wouldn't be able to get away. Hard to find temporary help during the holidays. Everyone wants to be with their families. Doc Benson is actually going to visit his daughter who moved to Arizona a few years back."

She could tell he was asking, in a non-asking way, why she was available.

"I didn't have anything special planned for the holidays." Nothing at all. Except avoiding them.

"Well, we're glad to have you. You let me know if you need anything while you're here. I left you a few things in the fridge to tide you over until you have time to shop."

"Yes, thank you. That was nice. I need my morning coffee."

"The coffee maker is on the counter. Filters in the drawer under the coffee maker."

"Miss Holly, I can help you with any chores or anything you need while you're here. I'm a good helper, aren't I, Dad?"

"You are, Josh. But I don't want you bothering Miss Holly."

"He's no bother. You're welcome any time, Josh."

The impish I-told-you-so grin Josh flashed at his dad almost made her break into laughter.

Wow. Laughing. When was the last time she'd laughed?

The boy's grin was almost a mirror image of his father's. He looked like a mini-twin to his dad. His dad had the same curly brown hair, only cut shorter. His broad shoulders filled out his chambray shirt. He had on the same simple jeans as his son, minus the rip in the knee. Work boots peeked out from the bottom of the jeans. Steve pushed off the porch, motioning for Louie to come. He turned to Josh who was busy stepping on and off the first step to the porch. "Come on, son. Let's let Miss Holly get all settled in."

Steve turned to Holly. "My phone number is written on the pad by the phone. Call me if you need anything."

"Thank you."

Holly watched the two of them walk away. Josh threw a stick and Louie chased after it. The three of them crossed the distance between the houses. She could just make out the shape of their house, faintly illuminated by the front porch light.

She rubbed her arms and looked around for the plug to unplug the Christmas lights. She saw Steve had put them on a timer. Okay. Fine. She'd leave them plugged in so she didn't mess up the timer and seem ungrateful for his efforts, but she didn't have to be happy with it.

She opened the door and went back inside to the cozy but lonely cottage if a place could be both cozy and lonely at the same time.

CHAPTER 2

The next day Holly arrived before the animal clinic opened but found the waiting room already filled with people and pets. She hadn't realized a clinic in such a small town would be so busy.

The girl at the front desk looked up with a cheerful smile. "May I help you?"

"I'm Holly Thompson. The temporary vet."

"Holly. Nice to meet you. I'm Julie. Doc Benson is in the back. Just head on down that way and he'll get you started."

Holly went down the hall and found Doc Benson sitting at a computer in the last room.

"Hi." Holly crossed into the room.

The man pushed back from the computer and stood up, holding out his weathered hand. "You must be Holly. Glad to have you here. You are my daughter's new best friend for covering for me over the holidays. She keeps asking me to come to Arizona for Christmas, but I never seem to be able to get away. Got two grandkids there, too. Will be nice to wake up on Christmas morning and see them open their gifts."

"Glad to be here."

"Hope you're not missing out on too much with your own family."

"No, I'm good. Didn't have anything planned."

The gray-haired man nodded. "I pulled up our schedule for today, and we'll just work it together this morning, then split up this afternoon. If you have any questions, just ask. I haven't scheduled any surgeries for the next two weeks, so you'd only have an emergency if one comes up."

"Sounds good."

"Hang your jacket up over there and we'll get started."

The morning raced by and Holly was surprised the first break they got was right before lunch when the people finally slowed down to a trickle.

Julie, from the front desk, offered to bring her

a sandwich from the Magnolia Cafe down the street and Holly gratefully accepted. She was going to have to go grocery shopping and stock up on a few things for while she was here. She usually packed a lunch to bring to work.

The afternoon was not quite as busy as the morning, but still a steady flow of people and pets. Doc Benson had a friendly and skilled vet tech, Cindy, and by the afternoon Holly felt confident that with Julie and Cindy's help, she could handle the practice while Doc Benson visited his daughter.

She stood at the front desk while Mrs. Black and her small poodle, Princess, checked out. The door to the clinic swung open and Josh and Louie burst into the waiting room.

"Hi, Miss Holly." The boy practically skipped across the waiting room.

"Hey, Josh. What's up?"

The boy looked at the floor, then back up to her. "Um, my dad wanted me to ask you to dinner tonight. We're having chili."

"Really? That would be nice. I still haven't had time to grocery shop."

"Sure. We usually eat about six-thirty. You can come over before that if you want."

"Tell your father thanks for the invitation."

"Uh, sure. I will."

Josh hightailed it out the door with a quick look back. It seemed like he couldn't wait to get away. Strange. She thought she'd hit it off last night with Josh.

Well, it would be nice to meet Josh's mom. It was kind of them to ask her over for dinner. She was tired after the stress of figuring out a new clinic and how things ran. She'd just stop by the corner market she saw this morning on her way to the clinic and pick up a few things. She'd grab a bottle of wine to bring as a thank you.

She soon found out she was not going to get wine at the corner market. They could only sell beer. She bought a six-pack of imported beer, hoping that would work. After grabbing a few essentials to tide her over for a few days, she headed back to the Christmas Cottage as she thought of it now.

Sure enough, as she pulled in the drive, the Christmas lights were glowing brightly, welcoming her home. The lights were the clear white kind, and she tried to convince herself some businesses had those kind of lights up all year round.

They're not really Christmas lights.

Holly decided to walk over to the Bergeron's house. It wasn't far and the fresh air brushed against her cheeks as she briskly walked over to their home, a six-pack cradled against her side. She stepped up on their front porch—another big porch with comfortable looking chairs and a swing—and rang the doorbell.

The door swung open and light tumbled out on the porch. Steve stood silhouetted in the light.

"Oh, hi, Holly."

"Hi, Steve."

He just stood there. Wasn't he going to ask her in?

"What brings you here?"

Huh? Hadn't he just invited her to dinner?

Josh slipped past his father and pulled on her hand. "Come in. We're just putting up the Christmas tree."

Steve stepped aside and let Josh pull her inside. She turned to Steve. "Here. I brought this." She shoved the six-pack into his hands. "I didn't know if you and your wife were beer drinkers, but I found out they don't sell wine at the market here."

Steve looked confused. "My wife?"

"I appreciate you asking me to dinner. I

haven't had much time to get things to cook. Not much on eating out every meal."

"Asking you to dinner?"

"Yes, I mean, Josh came by and said…" She looked at Steve's bewildered expression. It dawned on her, finally, that she'd made a mess of things. She should have known to check with the parents. *Always check with the parents*. She didn't even have kids but knew that rule. "You and your wife didn't ask me to dinner, did you?"

"Joshua."

Josh came back to stand in front of his father, scuffing his feet on the floor. "Did you invite Miss Holly to dinner?"

"I knew you always make enough chili for a bazillion people."

"Josh, you can't go asking people to dinner without telling me."

"I'm sorry, Dad. I just thought it would be fun to have her here. She can help decorate the tree."

The evening was just getting worse and worse.

"I'll just leave. I'm sorry for the mix-up." Holly started back out the door.

"No. No. Please come in. Of course you should stay for dinner."

"Don't you think you should clear it with Josh's mom?"

"I don't have a mom." Josh looked up at her with crystal clear blue eyes that held a hint of pain and a hint of defiance, daring her to question him.

"I..." Well, she couldn't make a bigger mess out of the night if she tried. "I'm sorry."

"Don't be. Josh and I get along just fine, don't we, bud?" His voice held a note of warning.

"Yep. We're bachelors." Josh flung his arms out wide. "This is our man house. And Dad is a great cook. So you'll stay?"

There was no way she could turn down that hopeful face turned up to look at her with questioning eyes. "Yes, I'll stay."

Josh grabbed her hand again. "Come on and help with the tree. We got all the ornament boxes out. Dad already got the lights on it."

There was no way to avoid this. She couldn't disappoint Josh. Though she'd rather clean the abscesses on a hundred animal wounds than decorate a Christmas tree.

"Grab an ornament and go for it." Steve pointed to the boxes. "Want a beer?" He lifted up the six-pack.

"Yes, that sounds good."

Steve opened the box, pulled out a bottle of beer and twisted off the top. "Glass?"

"No, bottle is fine." She took a good long swig of the cold liquid. Maybe for courage? She placed the bottle on a coaster on the coffee table and turned to the ornament box looming before her. Her hand shook as she reached into the box of ornaments and pulled out a small angel, covered with glitter.

"You okay?" Steve looked at her like he thought she was going to faint. Which, to be honest, she was darn near doing.

She sucked in a deep breath. "I'm fine." Good thing there wasn't a lie detector hooked up to her right now, the needle would be flipping out over her answer.

She slowly crossed over to the tree and reached up to an upper branch and carefully hung the angel. A light on the tree reflected on the small, delicate ornament. She stood and looked at it for a moment. This was not the way she'd pictured her Great Christmas Escape. Not at all.

Josh shuffled up beside her. "That's pretty. Look what I got." He held up a small sleigh with Santa sitting in it.

"That's a nice ornament, too."

Josh brought her each ornament before he hung them. Each. And. Every. One. She smiled and made the appropriate comment. Over and over.

Finally, Steve swung Josh up high to put an angel on the top of the tree.

"That means we're done decorating," Josh said as his father set him back down to the ground. "We always do the angel last. I get to do it."

"She's very pretty."

Josh looked at the tree with the critical eye of a child. "Yes, she is pretty. The tree looks great, Dad." He took another step back examining it carefully.

"Come on. Now we can have chili." Josh popped onto a new subject. Evidently the tree was finished and it was time to move on.

Yes, let's finish up this project and move on to normal life. Dinner. Conversation. Away from the tree.

"Dad always lets us eat in front of the Christmas tree on the night we decorate it."

Of course he did.

"That sounds nice," she lied. She lied big time.

"Josh, maybe we should eat in the kitchen. I don't think Miss Holly wants to sit on the ground and eat on the coffee table like we usually do."

"Sure she does."

Spoken with the confidence of a child.

"Yes, that's okay. I can sit on the floor."

"You sure? We do have a kitchen table." Steve tilted his head toward the kitchen.

"No, I'm sure."

They ate dinner under the traitorous Christmas tree. Josh chattered about his day, with Steve asking him a question here and there. Holly felt like she knew Josh's life story by the time dinner was over. Well, except for the part about not having a mother.

Steve stood up and took her empty bowl. "Josh, you go finish your homework while I clean up."

"Dad, I'll do it later." His Dad sounded like Daaaaad, at least two, if not three syllables.

"No, you know the rules. Finish the homework, then we'll see if there's time left for some TV."

"Fine." Josh got up and walked with a deliberate slow shuffle off in the direction she assumed was his room. He turned back around. "Hey Louie, come do homework with me." The dog got up from where he'd been sleeping under the tree and trotted off down the hall with Josh.

"Here, let me help." Holly got up from sitting

on the ground, but caught her toe on the leg of the coffee table and tumbled back down on her rear. *So graceful.*

"You okay?" Steve set down the bowls and knelt down beside her, his brown eyes filled with concern.

"Nothing hurt but my pride."

"I knew this was a bad idea. You were company, we should have eaten at the kitchen table."

"I was uninvited company and there was no reason to give up the tradition you have of dinner by the Christmas tree on the night you decorate it."

"Well, at least let me help you up." Steve stood up and reached out both his hands. His warm, strong hands, she soon found out. With a quick easy pull, he had her on her feet.

"Thanks. Now, let me help with the clean-up."

"You don't have to, you're a guest."

"Well, at least let me keep you company." Or maybe he wanted her to leave? After all it wasn't his idea for her to come to dinner or interrupt their father and son tree-decorating party.

"I'd like that. Come into the kitchen. I can put on a pot of coffee, or I could make you some tea. My momma was a tea drinker and I always keep it around. Don't know why. She passed on a couple of years ago. But I just feel like I need to have tea in the house." He looked like he'd said too much and turned to place the bowls in the sink.

"I'd love some tea, thank you." Interesting man. He was so gentle with his son and kept tea because his mother had been a tea drinker.

He put a kettle on the stove and cleaned up the kitchen while the water got hot. When the whistle sounded on the kettle, he pulled out a wooden box of tea bags. "Here, pick what you want."

She picked out a chamomile and Steve poured the hot water into a mug for her. "Sorry, I don't have a fancy teacup like Mom had. Just my coffee mugs."

"This is fine."

He came over and slid into the seat across from her at the table. He stretched his long legs out and bumped into her. "Oops, sorry. Not used to someone sitting across the table."

"That's okay."

She sipped on her tea. It was turning into a nice evening after all. Well, except for the whole Christmas tree thing. She debated whether she should ask about Josh's mom but decided it might be rude to ask.

"I didn't mean to cut you off when you were talking about Josh's mom."

So, he was a good chili maker and a mind reader too?

Steve shifted in his chair and picked up the salt shaker in front of him, twirling it around on the table. "Josh's mom left us when he was one. We were young. She wanted to put him up for adoption, but there was no way I could do that. I got sole custody and she moved on with her life. Josh asks about her sometimes, but he hasn't really ever known a life with a mom, so I think he's okay with it. He does as well as any kid without a mom."

"I'm so sorry. That must have been hard raising him alone."

"My momma was still alive then. She helped a lot. I don't know how I would have done it without her. My sister lived next door too then, and she helped out. Kind of the whole it-takes-a-village-to-raise-a-child scenario."

"You've done a great job. He's a wonderful kid."

"I think he is. He's just, well, he's great."

Holly put down her mug. "I guess I should be

going. I had a nice time. Glad you invited me." She grinned at him.

"Yes, it was a great idea of mine, wasn't it?" He grinned back at her then pushed back from the table. "We'll walk you home. Let me get Josh."

"There's no need for that."

"Humor me. I'd feel better if we escort you home."

They walked back into the family room and Steve called for Josh. The boy and the dog came trotting to the room.

"I finished my homework. Can I play now?"

"We're going to take Miss Holly home first, then a bath, then bed."

"Ooo-kaaay"

The three of them strolled out into the cool night. Josh ran ahead with Louie, throwing a stick and racing after the dog. They got over to her cottage and Steve stood on the porch while she unlocked the door. Louie came running up to the door, wagging his tail. She reached down to pet him. She stood back up and turned to Steve. "Thanks for tonight. I had a good time." And she realized she'd had a good time, even with the Christmas tree decorating ambush.

"See you soon." Steve stepped off the porch. "Come on Josh. Let's go."

"Bye, Miss Holly."

"Goodnight, Josh. Thanks for inviting me."

The boy turned and waved and raced off toward his house with Louie right at his heels. Steve lifted a hand in a half-wave of his own and followed the boy and the dog back toward his house.

She looked up at the night sky with millions of stars tossed across the darkness. A desolate quietness settled around her, an emptiness that reached to the depths of her soul. When would this aching, hollow feeling ever end? No matter what she did, or where she went, it chased her around like a relentless pack of wild wolves.

CHAPTER 3

"Miss Holly, Miss Holly." Josh came hurtling in the door to the animal clinic the next afternoon with Louie right beside him.

"Hi, Josh. What's up?" Holly had just finished up a busy day at the clinic. Her first one on her own. She thought she'd done pretty well, but she'd been glad to have the experienced vet tech, Cindy, who knew where everything was kept and most of the animals and their owners by name.

"I came to invite you to go to the tree lighting party tonight with me and my dad. They turn on all the lights and sing carols and the town council puts out hot chocolate and cookies." His invitation came out in a stream of words with barely a pause between them.

"Does your dad know you're asking me this time?"

"Yes, he does. Look." Josh pulled a wadded up piece of paper from his pocket and handed it to her.

If you'd like to join us tonight for the tree ceremony, we'll pick you up at the cottage at six. Thought you might like it in writing.

Holly grinned at Josh. "I see it's official then."

"Please come. Please?" Josh danced around from one foot to the other. Louie looked at her and wagged his tail as if pleading along with Josh.

The last thing she wanted was more Christmas festivities, but she didn't know how in the world she could turn Josh down. He pulled at her heart in ways it hadn't been pulled at in a long time. She'd been doing a good job this past year of keeping up walls and protecting her heart, but she couldn't bring herself to disappoint him. "Okay. I'll go with you."

"Yes." Josh did a success fist pump. "Come on, Louie, let's go tell Dad. See you tonight, Miss Holly." The boy and the dog left in a burst of energy and movement.

She finished up at the clinic and drove back to the cottage. She had just enough time to change into jeans and a sweater. Steve and Josh showed up at the cottage at exactly six. She grabbed a jacket and opened the door.

"Let's go, Miss Holly. This is going to be so much fun." Josh tugged at her hand, pulling her out the door. She smiled down at the boy. Life was just pretty exciting for him all the time. Well, except for the doing homework part.

They all climbed into Steve's truck with Josh and Louie in the back seat. They headed back into town. As they got near the city park that lined one side of a block on Main Street, she could see the crowd of people gathered. Steve parked the car and led the way over to the gazebo in the middle of the park. A couple of fires burned in scattered fire pits chasing away the bit of nip to the air. Steve placed his hand on her arm and led her over to where a group of people had gathered. Josh and Louie wove their way through the crowd and headed off to a cluster of kids by the swings.

"Hey, Steve."

A man came up to them and clapped a hand on Steve's back in the way that males did that she didn't really understand. Not quite a slap, not quite a punch, just a… clap.

"Ma'am." The man smiled at her.

"Gil, this is Holly. She's working Doc Benson's clinic while he's away for Christmas." Steve tilted his head toward the other man. "This is Gil Amaud. Good friend. Owner of the Feed and Seed."

"Nice to meet you, Gil."

"Good to meet you, too. I heard someone was working the clinic for Doc. Glad he got the chance to get away for a bit," Gil said.

Two women walked up to them, their arms laced together in an easy friendliness. "Hi." The red-haired woman reached up and kissed Gil's check.

"Hey, Sis."

"Holly, this is my sister, Bella, and her friend, Jenny."

"Hi." Holly smiled at the women, wondering how she was ever going to remember the names of all the people she'd met in the last few days.

"Where's Becky Lee?" Gil asked.

"She's working at Magnolia Cafe. A couple of waitresses are out with the flu, so she stayed to help Keely with the crowd they usually get after the tree lighting ceremony."

More names. Great.

"Bella, Jenny, and Becky Lee are like the unbreakable threesome around town. Have been since they were kids," Steve explained.

Holly just smiled and tried to keep everyone straight.

"We came early to help set up the hot chocolate and cookie table. We always help out with that." Jenny nodded towards the tables laden with cookies and big urns of hot chocolate.

Holly felt instantly welcome by the two women and the three of them chatted while the crowd milled around them. A few other people came up to them and Steve spent the evening introducing her to the town's people. More people. More names. More brothers, sisters, friends. After about the twentieth person, she gave up trying to keep everyone straight, but they were all very friendly to her.

Finally, the mayor came and stood on the raised gazebo. "Welcome. We're glad you could join us again this year." The mayor nodded to the high school band standing beside the gazebo and they began to play Silent Night. One by one the people around her joined in.

Holly stood and took in the sounds of the familiar carol, watching the faces of those around her. They all belonged. They all were enjoying time spent out with their friends. They were celebrating Christmas with friends and family. The exact thing she was trying to avoid this year, she reminded herself.

But still, the music and the smiles on everyone's faces pulled her back into the moment. Enjoying it even though she told herself she shouldn't. She couldn't. When the song ended there was a hush over the crowd. A dog barked once. She heard Josh's loud whisper. "Hush, Louie."

Then all at once, the large evergreen came alive with lights of every color and a brightly lit star on the top of the tree. A collective, ooooh went through the crowd.

Steve moved closer and smiled down at her. She shivered slightly from either the cool night air or from the emotions of the evening, she wasn't sure which.

"Cold?" Steve draped his arm lightly around her shoulder. She nodded and smiled. Forgetting for a moment she wasn't supposed to be enjoying herself. Enjoying anything that had to do with Christmas.

The band started up with Jingle Bells and the

crowd joined in. Holly relaxed and joined in the singing this time, too. After a few more carols, the mayor announced there were hot chocolate and cookies for everyone and motioned to the tables set up beside the gazebo.

"I'm going to go help serve." Bella touched Holly's arm. "It was nice meeting you."

"Nice meeting you, too."

The people of Comfort Crossing mingled around, sipping on hot chocolate and snacking on cookies. Steve introduced her to another hundred people. She'd swear it had been that many. He must know every single person in the town.

"Josh," Steve called out for his son a while later. Josh and Louie came running over. "We should go now. It's getting late."

The crowd broke up and people headed out to their cars. Josh and Louie led the way back to the truck, jumping over a low wall, and then walking down a bench on their way. The boy had boundless energy.

Until he didn't.

Josh nodded off to sleep on the way home.

They pulled into the drive at the cottage. Steve got out and walked around to open her door and help her out. He walked her up onto the front porch and took the key from her to open the door.

"I had a nice time." She smiled up at him, his dark brown eyes filled with a look that almost scared her. A look filled with friendship and caring and everything she didn't want. She took a step back, tripped on the doormat, and stumbled.

Steve reached out and caught her before she fell. His strong arm wrapped securely around her. Her heart beat faster and she told herself it was just from tripping, not from having this man holding her so close in his arms. Because that would be wrong.

"You okay?"

"I'm fine. Just clumsy, I guess." Holly pulled herself from his arms and the sudden lack of warmth startled her. Twice she'd fallen in front of him. He must think she was the biggest klutz.

"Well, goodnight then."

"Goodnight. Thanks again."

Steve looked at her for a moment, nodded, and turned to go back to his truck. She stood on the front porch and watched him pull out the drive. In a few moments, she could see the truck turning into the drive to the house next door.

She turned and walked into the cottage, and for one brief moment, before she could cram the thought safely out of sight, she wished she was going into the house with them. A house full of love and laughter. A family. All the things that were no longer hers. She deftly squashed those thoughts, from a year of practice, and closed the front door.

CHAPTER 4

Steve decided it would be neighborly to invite Holly to go for a drive. It was Sunday, the clinic was closed, and Josh was spending the night with a friend. The school winter break had started and Josh was off of school until after New Years.

Inviting Holly was only a friendly gesture, he promised himself. It wasn't the fact that he had enjoyed every minute he had spent with this woman. It wasn't her sexy smile, which he was pretty sure she had no idea she had, or her sparkling green eyes. It wasn't the way she tucked her brown hair back behind her ear when she looked down to talk to his son. He swore it wasn't any of those things just like it wasn't the fact he felt comfortable with her, unlike he had felt in a long time. Very long time.

He'd only dated a few women since Josh's mom had left. None of them had really amounted to anything. Well, except for Melissa. *And see how well that had turned out?*

Anyway, he was busy with work and raising Josh. Plus, he would never let another woman get close to Josh and then desert him. So he kept everything on a friendly level. Then, undoubtedly, the woman he was dating would get tired of being just friends and want more. They inevitably broke up. He'd repeated the pattern again. And again. Then he'd basically given up the whole dating thing.

But this wasn't a date. It was just a neighborly thing.

"Louie, let's go over to Miss Holly's and see if she wants to go for a drive." Louie slowly stretched and got up and crossed over to him. He reached down to pet the dog.

Louie was one creature they could depend on. He wasn't going to leave them. Steve was pretty sure that Louie thought Josh was the center of the universe which was exactly what Josh needed. Steve had adopted Louie from the local rescue group right after his Mom had died. Josh missed his grandmother, and the pup had been a great distraction.

Now Steve couldn't imagine life without the Aussie, with his quick wag, cheerful blue eyes, and energy to match Josh's. It was a good thing that Louie could match Josh's boundless energy because Steve knew he had a hard time keeping up with his son. What a spitfire. Not that he'd change one thing about Josh. Steve had been a carefree young man when Josh was born but from the moment Josh had looked up at him and wrapped his tiny fingers around his own, there had been nothing and no one that could have separated them. He'd matured quickly then, doing everything in his power to provide a good life for Josh.

They crossed the distance to the cottage with Louie loping ahead of him, then barging up on Holly's front porch and barking. Steve picked up his pace, trying to get to the front door. "Louie. Hush."

More barking. Well-behaved dog… until he wasn't.

The door opened and Holly came out on the porch. She was dressed in slim fitting jeans and a green sweater. Her hair was pulled back in a simple ponytail. She had on well-worn cowboy boots. Now he wouldn't have guessed that about her.

"Hi, Louie." Holly dropped to her knees and petted the dog. He licked her face and she laughed.

Steve finished the distance to the cottage. "Louie, polite dogs wait until I can get there and ring the doorbell, instead of barking up a storm. Sorry about that."

"It's not a problem."

"I was coming over to see if you wanted to go for a drive today. I have to go check on a job site. It's about twenty minutes away. Pretty drive, though. Thought you might like to get out for a bit."

"That does sound nice."

Good, she said yes. He was almost surprised. It had been so long since he had asked a woman out. Well, not out. *This was just a drive.*

"Josh is at a friend's house and is spending the night. So it will just be us and Louie."

"If you come in, I could be ready to go in just a few minutes. I'll walk back over with you."

"Okay. Louie, you stay."

"It's okay with me if he comes in if it's okay with you."

"Okay, Louie. But you be on good behavior." The dog trotted inside.

"There's coffee on if you want to pour yourself a cup. I'll be ready in a jiff."

He crossed into the kitchen and pulled a mug from the cupboard. He filled the mug and took a long swig of the dark brew. Good stuff. She liked strong coffee, too.

He lounged against the counter while he waited for Holly to get ready. He looked out the window to the grove of pecan trees. They were finally getting bigger. His sister had planted them when she first bought the house. Well, he'd helped her plant each and every one of them, but she'd always insisted she planted them and they were her grove. They still didn't yield much in the way of pecans, but he figured they would in time.

He missed having his sister living next door. It had been a couple of years since she moved away. She usually came back for Christmas, but this year she'd said her work schedule was crazy, and she hoped to come back in January. It would be a small Christmas this year with just him and Josh.

Holly came into the kitchen. He could see she'd put on a touch of makeup and had a jacket with her. "I'm ready to go."

He took the last gulp of coffee, rinsed the mug, and slipped it into the dishwasher.

Holly flashed him an appreciative smile. “Nice quality in a male.”

“What?”

“The ability to know where a dishwasher is and how to use it.”

He smiled back at her. “Just one of my many talents.”

Holly settled back into the surprisingly comfortable seat in the truck. She’d thought that trucks were hard and manly and rough driving. Not this one. It had a small back seat and Louie sat back in it. The inside of the cab had a clipboard on the front seat, a hammer, and a tape measure. All of which Steve had thrown into the back seat.

She was glad she’d said yes to this outing. An excursion that had nothing, absolutely nothing, to do with Christmas.

“This is a really nice house we’re building. Set up on a small ridge that overlooks a little creek running through the back of the property. The guy we’re building it for is picky down to the last little detail, but I’m pretty much that way myself. I like to go out and check on it a couple of times a week."

"Do you just build one house at a time?"

"I have four houses going up right now. Getting ready to start the fifth. Hoping the weather stays nice for a while so we can get the foundation poured."

"Do you like owning your own construction company?"

"I do. I really enjoy seeing the houses go up. It's kind of tight and uncertain at times when the economy tanks, but I rode out the last slump all right. Glad things have picked back up and hope they stay that way for a long time."

"How did you get into the construction business?"

"I'd been helping my uncle with his business since I was about fourteen. I kept working there after school and during the summer. I started college, but then… well, I just drifted around a bit. Then Josh was born, I came back here to Comfort Crossing, and started working full time for my uncle."

"It must have been hard working full time and raising Josh."

"It was. I was so darn tired. So tired that sometimes I could barely see straight."

Holly hid a smile at his obvious embarrassment for letting a swear word slip out. She wasn't going to tell him that she knew a few curse words herself.

"Anyway, Mom and my sister helped out a lot. We got through it. Since my office is in town, Josh comes there after school, then rides with me if I need to go out to a job site. Or he plays in the park now that he's older. It's gotten a little easier."

"What do you do for fun or for hobbies?" Holly found herself wanting to know more and more about Steve and Josh. Why? That wasn't the way to stay detached, she chastised herself silently.

"Fun is anything I do with Josh. I don't really have a hobby, just no time for it."

Steve turned onto a narrow country road. "So, how did you get into wanting to be a vet?"

"I've been crazy about dogs since probably the day I was born. It expanded to other animals. Then I worked for a vet in the summers in high school. I was hooked."

"So is someone watching your pets for you while you're here?"

Holly sucked in a quick breath. "I don't have any pets." Not any more. She hoped she would be able to again sometime, but right now it was out of the question.

He sent her a quizzical look.

She knew people thought it weird she didn't have a dog or a cat. She didn't so much as have a fish this year.

Tears began to well in her eyes and she turned to look out the window, fighting off the tears with an effort she'd perfected this last year.

"You okay? I say something wrong?"

Holly slowly sucked in a deep breath and turned toward Steve. "I lost my dog a while ago. I'm not ready for another one." Her beloved dog wasn't all she'd lost. The pain rolled over her again. She thought she'd learned to handle things, but at unexpected moments it all came crashing back on her.

"I'm sorry."

"Yes, me too." She'd lost everything that Christmas on that fateful snowy night.

She was grateful to see Steve pull into a dirt driveway in front of an almost-built house. The siding was on it, and the roof. The windows had stickers on them, and a long plank led up to the front door where the steps hadn't been added yet.

Steve turned off the truck and looked over at her. He reached out and placed his hand over hers that was resting on the truck seat. "You ready to go inside?"

His hand was rough and warm. Strangely gentle for such a large hand. Yes, she was ready. She wanted out of the truck and into the fresh air, away from her thoughts.

"Yes, let's go. I can't wait to see it."

He came around and helped her down from the truck. He kept her hand gently in his as they walked to the house. She liked that. Her hand in his. As soon as she realized she liked it, she slipped her hand free. None of that nonsense. They were here to see the house. That was all. There was no way she was going to enjoy his hand, or his smile, or that look he tossed at her sometimes that made her knees go weak. Nope, she was stronger than that.

But as he took her hand to help her up onto the porch, she left her hand in his this time. Gosh, she was a weak, weak woman.

CHAPTER 5

They drove back toward Comfort Crossing, but Steve didn't want the day to end. As they got closer to town, he thought of ways to delay taking her back to the cottage.

"I had a nice time today. Kind of sorry to see it end." Steve smiled at Holly.

"I could make dinner for you if you like," Holly offered.

"That would be great." It would be great. The day wouldn't end and he could spend some more time with her.

It had been a wonderful afternoon as far as he was concerned. He had loved showing Holly the house he was building. She'd asked questions and eagerly looked at every little detail in the house. He admitted, only to himself, that it had been a big pump to his ego when she'd admired so many things. She loved the detailing on the woodwork. She'd commented on the light fixtures and the massive stone fireplace. He knew he hired good subcontractors and expected the highest quality out of them, and she seemed to know and appreciate the craftsmanship.

"If we swing by the market, I'll pick up a few things. Spaghetti sound all right?" Holly interrupted his thoughts.

It sounded fantastic to him. She could have offered bread and water. He was just glad for the invite. "Yep, spaghetti sounds great."

They popped into the market and picked up the things she needed for dinner.

"I'm going to get this," Steve said as they got up to the checkout.

"No, you don't have to do that."

"I insist. You cook, I buy."

She flashed that sexy smile at him again and he almost dropped his wallet.

They arrived at the cottage just at dusk. The Christmas lights blinked on as they pulled in the drive. He heard Holly take a sharp intake of air. He looked at her, but she was looking straight out the side window now. She was a hard one to figure out. A bit touchy and he didn't know why he seemed to always be pushing her buttons. He needed to figure them out and learn to take a wide detour around them.

He parked the truck and grabbed the groceries. She'd already climbed out of the truck by the time he had come around to help her. Louie ran ahead of them and up the steps to the porch.

They followed Louie to the porch and inside. Steve reached over and flipped the switch to light up the family room. They crossed to the kitchen and Steve placed the groceries on the counter.

"Okay, don't give me an apron, but I'll help with making the dinner." He smiled at Holly, hoping to tease out one of her grins. He was rewarded for his efforts.

"Well, I'm from the school of cooking that says you always need to wear an apron, but we'll make an exception for you this time."

She proceeded to boss him around with instructions for making the salad while she worked on the meat sauce and boiled the spaghetti. He obediently followed her directions, though he was perfectly able to make a salad on his own, for Pete's sake. But he liked her silly orders and they laughed as they made dinner.

While the sauce was simmering, she pulled out a bottle of red wine. "Want some?"

"Yes. Sounds good."

They sat at the kitchen table and sipped wine. Holly asked more questions about the house they'd seen and about his construction business. He noticed she much preferred talking about his life instead of hers.

Louie barked at the back door. Steve pushed away from the table and stood up. "Need to go out, Louie?" He opened the back door and let Louie outside. Steve stood there for a minute and Louie came busting back inside, sat at Steve's feet and looked at him expectantly. "Good boy. Sorry, don't have any treat for you, bud." Louie looked at him skeptically and crossed over to sit at Holly's feet, obviously disappointed in Steve.

Steve closed the door. "It's getting a little bit chilly outside. Want me to start a fire for you?"

"That would be nice. Why don't you do that while I finish up dinner?"

Steve went outside to the woodpile and grabbed an armload of logs. He quickly had a fire going with the help of a few fire starters and rolled newspaper. He carefully replaced the screen. He'd just let the fire get going while they ate.

Holly had the table set and food on the table when he returned to the kitchen. “Smells great.” He crossed over to the kitchen sink and washed his hands. He grabbed the bottle of wine and put in on the table.

“Well, let’s eat.” Holly slipped into the chair he had pulled out for her. Small locks of her hair had fallen out from her ponytail and circled her face, rosy pink from the heat of the stove. She shoved them away with a flick of her hand, but they drifted back. He liked the way the disheveled curls framed her face.

He sat down at the table and they both reached for the bowl of spaghetti at the same time. Their hands brushed and Holly pulled hers back quickly.

“No, you go first.” Steve insisted.

He watched her skillfully dish up spaghetti noodles without dropping any stragglers along the way. He wasn’t so lucky when he took his turn.

They ate and talked and sipped wine and he had a wonderful time. Holly seemed to relax more as the evening wore on. She surprised him with her dry humor and quick laugh. Her eyes sparkled as she teased him.

He helped her with the dishes after dinner showing, once again, he knew how to use a dishwasher. He dried off the big pot she'd used to boil the spaghetti and tucked it away under the counter.

He grabbed the bottle of wine and they went to sit in front of the fire. The family room had warmed up nicely from the cheerful fire. They lounged on the couch and continued their friendly banter. He couldn't remember when he'd had such a fun and relaxing time with a woman.

Louie jumped up on the couch beside Holly. "Is that okay? Is he allowed on the furniture?"

"Okay by me, if it's okay with you."

Holly scooted closer to Steve to give Louie more room. She ran her fingers through Louie's thick fur. The dog stretched out more, and she found herself smack up against Steve as she gave the dog more room. The dog slowly closed his eyes and gave a big sigh as she petted him. She was torn between totally immersing herself in how good it felt to have a dog curled up beside her again or trying to ignore how right it felt and how much she'd missed it.

"You okay?" Steve's voice was deep and

warm. He had a sneaky way of being in tune to her feelings. She wasn't sure she liked it.

"Yes, I'm fine." She then realized she was fine. She was tired of hiding and pushing thoughts and memories away. She petted Louie again, and he gave one lazy tail thump on the couch.

"You want to talk about it?" Steve's tone questioned but didn't really pry.

She realized, and it surprised her, that she did want to talk about it. She hadn't really talked to anyone about it since it happened.

Since the funeral.

"It was last Christmas." She wasn't sure she could tell what happened, but she was going to try. For the first time ever. Lynn had always been her buffer. Explaining what had happened. Making phone calls. Being her front man—woman. Holly took a deep, steadying breath, her heart racing.

"We had a bad snow and ice storm. My husband, Dave and our dog, Tucker, were coming home from the hardware store. Dave wanted to put up more Christmas lights, and I told him it was silly to get out on the roads, but he insisted. Wanted our house to be all fixed up for Christmas. His parents were coming and we had just bought the house." The familiar surge of pain washed over her and she had to stop and just breathe.

Steve waited patiently for her to continue.

Holly stared into the fire as the memories of that night came rushing back. "Dave was taking a long time, and I was starting to get worried. I stood at the window for such a long time. Wishing him to show up. I finally saw headlights in the drive, but it was the police. Dave had been killed instantly by a driver who lost control on the slick roads. Then they told me that Tucker was injured and was taken to the vet clinic. My vet clinic. The police drove me there. I so wanted to save Tucker, to save one of them, and the other vet—my best friend, Lynn—and I worked on Tucker. We just couldn't save him. I lost both of them that night."

Holly threaded her hand through Louie's thick fur, burying her fingers in its warmth. "I was just numb by then. No tears. Just… so… tired. Lynn took me home to her house, and I stayed there for days while she made all the arrangements."

She turned and looked at Steve. His eyes held compassion and a knowing about loss. "My husband, Dave, was a vet, too. We worked together. After he… was gone… it was so hard everywhere. At home, at work. There was no escape. I sold the house and moved into an apartment. But I couldn't avoid my work. He was still everywhere at work. I could picture him smiling at me in passing. The great way he had with the animals. I could hear his laugh. He was such a good man. I loved him so much. And Tucker. I missed them both so much. Everything was just so empty after that."

"I'm so sorry, Holly."

"Thank you." She fell silent then, not sure what else to say. Hot tears trailed down her cheeks and she dashed her palms at them to wipe them away. It felt almost good, in a very strange way, to have finally spoken about that night. Cleansing in a way. She leaned against the back of the couch and stared into the dancing flames in the fireplace.

"So that's why you're not very big into Christmas this year."

"I thought if I came here to Comfort Crossing, I could just avoid the holiday this year."

"But Josh and I went and decorated your cottage. And Josh invited you over to help decorate our tree. Oh, and let's not forget we invited you to the tree lighting ceremony. I'm sorry. I had no idea."

"That's okay. It was hard at first, especially

when I first drove up to the cottage and saw all those Christmas lights. But, really, how can you not get caught up in Josh's enthusiasm for the holidays? And who could help falling for Louie?"

The dog opened his eyes at the sound of his name and looked at her with a knowing, old soul glance. The dog pressed against her. Steve wrapped his arm around her and drew her close against him.

"Louie is a big pig when it comes to sharing a couch." Steve grinned down at her.

"I can see that."

Holly took another big breath and let it out slowly. For the first time in she couldn't remember how long, she felt relaxed. She'd go so far as to say she felt content. It had been such a long, long time.

Steve's warmth and the heat from the fire comforted her like sleeping under an old quilt. Lulling her. Calming her. She relaxed against Steve and he gently put his hand on hers.

CHAPTER 6

Steve looked down at Holly sleeping peacefully tucked up against his side. She'd endured so much in the last year. Losing her husband, then adding on to that the loss of her dog, Tucker. No wonder she'd come to Comfort Crossing to hide out this holiday season.

His breath got in a rhythm with her breathing. He tightened his arm around her shoulder. He'd give anything to take away her pain and felt horrible he'd thrown Christmas at her at every turn.

She sighed in her sleep. The firelight flicked flashes of light across her face. She was a beautiful woman with strong cheekbones and long eyelashes that lined her now-closed emerald eyes.

He let the warmth wash over him and held

her tightly against him, hoping that telling him about last Christmas would somehow release the stranglehold the memories held over her. Let her move on with her life instead of hide away from the pain.

He knew about hiding away from pain and loss. One day, you just had to pick up and move on. No matter how hard it was.

The next thing he knew he was lying on the couch with Holly curled up against him. Louie was on the floor and the fire was dying. He glanced at the clock and saw it was the middle of the night. Should he extract himself and go home? That might wake her up. How had they gotten from sitting up on the couch to stretched out flat against each other, her one leg was entwined in his? He really had no desire whatsoever to get up. It was cold outside. Excuse one. He didn't want to wake her, she needed her sleep. Excuse two. She just felt so good up against him. Well, that was probably the most honest excuse.

He could feel her heart beat against his chest. Her hair was mostly pulled out of the clip she'd used to pull back her hair, and it fell in silken locks across his shoulder.

She stirred and he held his breath, willing her

not to wake up. He must have done something right with the karma police because she settled back up against him. He really hoped she stayed asleep. Or maybe he wanted her to wake up.

It was quite a while before he felt himself begin to drift back to sleep.

Then he was wide awake because Holly stirred and kissed his neck.

Oh, sweet keeper of the stars, he was cold-shower awake now. He kissed the top of her head, knowing full well she was still asleep.

He figured he'd just stay here, tortured, for the rest of the night. He didn't want to wake her. Didn't want to scare her off. But he sure as all get-out didn't want to leave.

Holly slowly woke up, trying to figure out where she was. Then, bang, she knew. She was lying almost on top of Steve, who was snoring quietly. She tried to untangle herself… one of her legs was locked firmly between his. As she moved, he tightened his arm around her.

Just great. She needed to get up before he woke up and found out they were hopelessly entangled. How did this happen?

Last night slowly came back to her. Telling Steve about Dave and Tucker. Steve had been so understanding and let her take her time to tell it all. She felt like a weight had been lifted this morning. Like she could go on and face each day now.

But she didn't want to face Steve like this. On the couch. Curled up around him.

She started to pull away, slowly and carefully.

"Hm," Steve growled a friendly rumble. "Morning."

"Morning. I'm sorry. I guess I fell asleep." She tried to slide her leg out from between his.

"Looks like we both did." He stretched slightly, and she felt herself go along for the ride, plastered against his hip.

She did manage to pull her leg out this time and pushed up to a sitting position.

He looked quite content, stretched out on the couch, grinning up at her. The beast.

"What are you smiling at?" She tugged the clip out of her hair and raked her fingers through the mess, sure she looked a fright.

"You look darn sexy in the morning."

She had no words.

He pushed up and swung his legs to the floor.

He reached over and tucked a lock of her hair behind her ear. And grinned at her again.

She self-consciously straightened her sweater.

He reached out and touched her cheek then. Just a brush of his hand.

"I better go," he said. In that low sexy voice of his. Maddening voice. Teasing voice.

"About last night. Thanks for listening to me." She reminded herself to keep from getting lost in his dark brown eyes.

"Glad you felt you could talk to me." His morning voice was deeper than his day voice. Richer. Warmer.

She got up then, reluctant for the night to end. Louie got up from his place in front of the fire and barked.

"He needs to go out." Steve pushed off the couch. "Come on, Louie. Let's head home."

She walked him to the door, and he stopped for a moment as he was leaving. "I had a good time yesterday."

"I did, too."

"Do you want to come over for dinner after work? Josh is cooking. I let him cook every once in a while. He's making grilled cheese and mac and cheese. His choice. I'm sure he'd love to show off for you. Want to come over?"

"That sounds like fun. Can I bring anything?"

"Nope, it's all up to Josh. Well, with a bit of help. See you about six?"

"See you then."

She watched the man and the dog head back over to his house in the early morning light. The sky was a rosy pink color in the clouds to the east. A new day, and for once, in a very long time, she felt like she was ready to face it head-on.

CHAPTER 7

Josh threw open the door when Holly arrived promptly at six. "Miss Holly. I'm making dinner, did Dad tell you? I'm a great cook."

He tugged on her hand and pulled her into the house. "Dad, you should hang up her jacket. Miss Holly, come into the kitchen and watch me cook."

Holly smiled at the boy's enthusiasm. She obediently gave her jacket to Steve and followed Josh to the kitchen, winking at Steve as she handed him the jacket. Louie followed in their wake.

"See, I made bread. I used the bread machine."

"That's great, Josh."

"I'm going to make the grilled cheese. The macaroni is boiling, see? Dad drains the macaroni. He won't let me do it myself, but I did everything else." Josh stood up on a stool by the counter in front of an electric sandwich grill. He carefully spread butter on the bread, piled on the cheese and buttered the top slices of bread. He placed the sandwiches on the grill and closed the lid.

When the light went off on the sandwich maker, Josh speared the sandwiches with a fork. "I have to make more. You guys sit down. Dad, can you put the macaroni and cheese on the table?"

Steve grabbed the mac and cheese and placed it on the hot pad on the table. He held out the chair for her and she slipped into her seat.

"Wine?" Steve held up a bottle of red.

"Yes, please."

Steve poured them both wine and a glass of milk for Josh while the boy finished up the sandwiches. Josh carried the plate of sandwiches to the table and placed it in the center of the table with a flourish.

Josh and Steve took their seats. "Okay, let's eat. I hope you like it, Miss Holly."

She did like it. She complimented Josh on both

the toasted cheese sandwiches and the mac and cheese. Josh grinned for most of the meal, explaining each step of the process of making their dinner. "The secret to good mac and cheese is I use three kinds of cheeses," Josh whispered to her.

"Tell you what, Josh. Since you cooked, I'll do the dishes. Why don't you go out and turn on the TV? We'll be out as soon as I finish up." Steve pushed back from the table.

"Okay." Josh left the kitchen and in a moment she could hear the noise of a television program coming on.

"Let me help." Holly began to stand up and clear the table.

"Nope. You sit there and drink your wine. I've got this."

She sank back into the chair. It had been a long day at the clinic. She thought she was getting more into the groove of working at Comfort Crossing Animal Clinic, but it was still not as familiar as working at her own vet clinic. It felt good to be off her feet.

"Good day at work?" Steve asked.

"It was good. I'm still learning the system there though. They have a different computer system, but the girls there help me with that. They find things I need. It's going fine, I'm just tired today."

"So is Josh. I'm not sure he got much sleep at all at his so-called sleepover."

She wasn't sure she'd gotten much sleep last night and she'd bet Steve hadn't either.

Steve finished the dishes, and they grabbed their glasses of wine to go out and join Josh. He was sound asleep on the couch. Steve turned off the TV, scooped up his son, and disappeared down the hall with him. The sight pulled at her heart, Steve with his son safely curled up in his arms. He was such a good father. Always thinking of Josh, what was right for him.

She sank down onto the overstuffed couch and wanted to put her tired feet up on the coffee table, but didn't. The fire danced in the fireplace and the warmth from it comforted her. It was so homey and relaxed at Steve and Josh's home. Everything about the house said come in and sit down. Relax. The house was picked up and organized, but you could tell a boy lived here. A baseball bat rested beside the front door. A video game player was connected to the TV. There was a shelf full of kids' books on the bookshelf across the room.

Steve came back into the room and sat down

beside her. "He was out. So tired. He barely woke up when I put on his pajamas. Poor little guy. He loves to go to sleepovers, but it takes like two days for him to recover."

"He really did a great job on dinner."

"He did, didn't he? He loves to learn to cook. I try to let him do his own meal every week or so. He loves to help me cook, too."

"He is such a great kid."

Steve smiled at her. "I think so."

They sat in quiet, watching the fire. Louie jumped up on the couch, just like last night, claiming his space. She scooted over to give the dog room, and Steve wrapped his arm around her and pulled her closer to him.

She was totally enjoying the moment. Louie, with his head in her lap. The fire. And Steve. Steve with his arm around her shoulder and his other hand covering hers.

Steve pulled back slightly and turned to her. He brought his hand up, tilted her chin, leaned down and at that very moment she knew he was going to kiss her.

Only she didn't want him to, didn't want to ruin this perfect moment.

Only she did want him to kiss her. Only she shouldn't want it. Only…

He cut off her thoughts when his lips came down upon hers. A questioning kiss that deepened as she offered no resistance. His warm hand framed her face. She kissed him back, she couldn't help herself. Her hand slipped up to his chest and she could feel his heart beating. He pulled her closer. She felt her breath grow ragged. His lips were hard and soft at the same time. How could that be? His uneven breathing matched her own.

What was she doing?

She pulled back, waking up Louie who opened his eyes, shot her a look of annoyance, if a dog could do that, and got up and went to curl up by the fire.

Steve looked at her questioningly.

Her breath was still uneven and the air between then held a viable tension. "I…" She took a deep breath. "I need to go."

"Wait." Steve placed his hand on her arm, stopping her from leaping off the couch like she'd planned. "You okay?"

"I'm fine," she lied. A lie was a good move here. She stood up and went to grab her jacket.

Steve levered himself off the couch and followed her to the door.

"Holly. I'm sorry. I didn't mean to—"

She cut him off. "No need to be sorry. I just

need to get home. Big day tomorrow at the clinic. Tell Josh thanks for making my dinner."

She fled out the door. Running away from Steve. From his kiss. From his warmth. From her mixed up emotions.

She briefly glanced back when she made it over to the cottage and saw Steve illuminated by the Christmas lights on his house. Standing there watching her escape.

Steve stood on Holly's front porch first thing in the morning the next day. He knocked on her front door. He'd tossed and turned all night, going over every second of the evening. He knew he'd scared her with the kiss, just as much as he knew in his heart she had wanted it, that she'd felt it as deeply as he had. Maybe she wasn't ready. Maybe she was and felt guilty. He wasn't sure. But one thing was sure, he was going to confront her right now instead of leaving the awkwardness hanging between them.

The door opened and Holly stood there with a cup of coffee in her hand. She was fully dressed, down to the shoes, but she looked adorably just-morning sleepy. Or maybe she'd tossed all night like he had.

"Holly. Can we talk?"

She nodded and moved back to let him in.

"Why did you run off?" Though he knew darn well why she had.

"I didn't run off. I just needed to get home."

"You weren't in a hurry to get home before I kissed you."

"I— "

She looked at him with those green eyes. The ones that had haunted his dreams last night. What little he had dreamed.

"It was… I wasn't…." She looked down at the coffee cup wrapped in her delicate hands. "Yes, I ran. I'm sorry."

"No need to be sorry. I just wanted to make sure you're okay. That we're okay."

"I've had a good time with you. With you and Josh. I just haven't been with—been close to—another man except for Dave for so many years. It's only been a year since he's been gone…"

"But you felt something, the same thing I felt. I know you did."

"I did. But I'm not sure I want to." She was still avoiding his eyes and staring at her coffee cup like it held the answer to the meaning of life.

He reached over and tilted her face up to look at him. "It's okay to let go. You're not betraying him. You'll always have his memory and your time together."

"It's too soon."

"We can't always pick the time when someone comes into our lives and we start caring about them. Sometimes it just happens. Maybe not at the perfect time… but in its own time."

"I know. I just…" She sighed and turned away from him and crossed over to look out the front window. "I wasn't expecting this. I came here to avoid Christmas, to hang out and just make it through the holidays. Things aren't going as I planned. This isn't what I wanted."

"But it's there, isn't it? You have feelings, too."

"I feel… something. I admit."

"Holly, look at me. Please."

She slowly turned around to face him, a cautious look on her face.

He moved a step closer to her. "I do have feelings for you. I know it happened quickly. I wasn't expecting it either, but it's the truth. I'd like to get to know you better. See where things go. Will you give it a chance?" Steve stood there, waiting for an answer, hoping she would be willing to give them some time, to see where things were headed with them.

She stood there for the longest time. He was sure she was going to shoot him down. His heart pounded in his chest, waiting for her answer.

"I'll try. I don't make any promises though. I still don't feel very steady on my feet. My life has been such a roller coaster. I was hoping for dull and boring these holidays."

"It's been anything but that, hasn't it?" He grinned at her.

She smiled then. That gorgeous, sexy smile that lit up her eyes to the shade of emeralds. "It's not been boring, I'll give you that."

"Josh is nuts about you, too. You're all he talks about. Miss Holly said this. Louie loves Miss Holly. Can we have Miss Holly over for dinner?"

"I'm kind of nuts about him, too. He's great."

"So, it's settled then. No more running away." He nailed her with his gaze.

"I'll try. That's all I can give you."

"I'll take it."

After a busy morning at the veterinary clinic, Holly was glad for a break for lunch. She grabbed her jacket and cell phone and decided to go walk to the city park. She needed to call her best friend, Lynn, and talk. Boy did she need to talk.

She walked to the park and sat on one of the benches. She dialed her friend's cell phone number, hoping Lynn had time to talk now, too.

Lynn picked up on the second ring. "Holly! So glad to hear from you. How's it going on the great escape?"

Her friend's voice was full of warmth and familiarity. She'd missed Lynn. She was used to seeing her almost every day at work. "Well, the whole escape thing? Not so much."

"What's wrong?"

"It's not so much wrong as..." How did she explain this? "It's not working out like I planned. First I met Louie, he's the most gorgeous merle Aussie dog. Then I met his owner, Josh. He's an eight-year-old boy. Then I met his dad, Steve."

"Well, this is a story I want to hear."

"It's been Christmas this, and Christmas that. Oh, and the cottage I'm staying at? Yep, all decorated for Christmas. Lights. Red bows. You name it. It's like it's the official Christmas cottage."

"I'm sorry. You doing okay?"

"I'm getting used to it."

"So, get back to the boy, the dog, and the dad."

"I'm getting there. Steve is a builder. He does great work. I went with him to see one of the homes he's building. It was the most fabulous house. And his son is such a great kid. So cute. Well-behaved in an all-boy kind of way. He's a force to be reckoned with. I'm defenseless to say no to anything he asks."

"More on the dad."

Holly smiled. Her friend wanted to get down to the real reason for the call. "He's nice."

"Nice? That's all you're going to give me? You can do better than that. What's he look like?"

"He's tall. Dark brown hair and eyes. The most mesmerizing smile. His voice is, oh, I can't even describe it. Deep. Sexy. Kind. And, Lynn—he kissed me."

"Ah, so that's what this is about."

"It was a good kiss. A great kiss. But then I ran."

"That's okay. Just go run back."

"But I feel guilty. Like I'm cheating on Dave. I even feel like I'm cheating on Tucker because I'm really crazy about Josh's dog, Louie."

"Holly, it's been a year. You've hidden away every darn day of it. You have every right to be happy. Dave would have wanted that. Heck, Tucker would have wanted that. You don't have to live in the past."

"I know. But it all happened so fast. I wasn't expecting it."

"Love comes in its own time."

"Steve said almost the same thing. But didn't use the word love."

"But he cares about you?"

Holly nodded even though Lynn obviously couldn't see her. "I think he does."

"You care about Steve?"

"I think I do. No, I do. He's amazing. You should see him with Josh. He's a single dad and has done such a great job raising his son."

"Wow, Holls, I just love hearing your voice sounding like this. I think I'm brilliant for finding you this temporary job for Christmas. No, it's okay. You can thank me later."

"It has been good to get away. Away from the clinic where Dave worked. I miss you tons though."

"Miss you, too. Hey, just a sec."

Holly heard Lynn talking to someone in the background.

"Holls, I gotta run. Puppy who ate a plastic Christmas ornament just arrived. Call me soon.

Keep me updated. Oh, and Holls? Don't feel guilty. Feel happy."

Holly slipped the phone into her coat pocket. A peace settled over her. She felt better. Much better. Talking to Lynn always helped her sort her feelings out.

CHAPTER 8

"Miss Holly. Miss Holly." Josh rushed into the clinic right before closing. Louie, of course, was right at his heels. "I told my dad we should get you a Christmas tree. You don't have one. That's not right. Everyone has a Christmas tree."

Steve came into the clinic, obviously trying to keep up with the boy and Louie. He smiled at her and her heart did a little flutter. A flutter like she hadn't felt in ever so long. She felt her face break into a smile right back at him.

"Slow down, Josh. Give Miss Holly a chance to talk." He turned from the boy, back to her. "Would that be okay with you? A tree?"

The beginnings of resistance tugged at her but, to her surprise, the feeling just melted away.

She was helpless to resist the boy. "I think that would be lovely."

"You sure?" Steve cocked one eyebrow.

She knew Steve was aware of her original hide-from-the-holidays plan, but he probably hadn't been able to resist Josh's pleas either.

"I'm sure."

"Tonight? Can we do it tonight?" The boy danced from one foot to the other. Louie gave one quick bark.

"Okay. That sounds good."

"Yes. Hear that, Louie? We're doing another tree tonight."

The dog wagged his tail in answer.

"Hey, look what I taught Louie." The boy ping-ponged onto another subject. "Sit. Down. Sit. Down." The dog obediently followed the commands. "Now watch this! Roll over." The dog rolled over then jumped up.

"That's great, Josh."

"Okay. We'll be over tonight." Jumping again on his subjects. "Come on, Dad. We have to get the tree." The boy tugged at his father's hand.

Steve turned to her. "My sister has lights and ornaments stored in the closet in the back room. We'll use those. Six-thirty okay? I'll pick up something for us to eat. Sandwiches from The Magnolia Cafe."

"Sounds good."

She watched Steve and his mini clone walk out the door. Josh was looking up at his dad and chattering away. She smiled. Decorating a tree. She couldn't believe she was not only going to have a tree this Christmas, but she was looking forward to it.

Steve and Josh entered the Christmas tree yard beside his friend Gil Amaud's hardware store, The Feed and Seed. Gil kept the town supplied with a plethora of trees and evergreen roping each Christmas. The lot was decorated with brightly lit trees at the entrance and big red bows tied along the temporary split rail fencing lining the lot. Christmas music drifted through the air from an old boombox—no fancy MP3 player here.

Gil always had a big urn of hot chocolate for the shoppers. His sister, Bella, often dropped off plates of Christmas cookies. The Feed and Seed had been in their family for years.

"I'm going to go look at the big ones over there." Josh pointed and headed off with Louie.

"Hey, didn't I already sell you a tree at a bargain price?" His friend walked up and clapped him on the back.

"That you did. It's already up and decorated. But I'm picking one up for Holly."

"Ah, the fill-in vet for Doc Benson. The one you introduced me to at the tree lighting ceremony. I heard you've been hanging out with her."

"We've just had her over a few times."

"Which is a few more times than you've had any other female over in years." Gil pinned him with a don't-deny-it look. "You like her, huh?"

"I might. A bit." Steve felt a sheepish, goofy, grin creep across his face.

Gil laughed out loud. "So, she's got you under her spell? Well, good for her. I thought you were going to avoid all women after—what was her name—Mary, Mindy, Molly…"

"Melissa."

"Ah, yes. That was it. I figured when she dumped you that was the last straw with you and women."

It had been. For a long time. Melissa had patiently explained to him—after a year of dating

—that while she had a good time with him, he was too busy with his son and really, couldn't he just leave Josh with a sitter every weekend so they could go out more?

Like that was ever going to happen.

Josh was his whole life. He enjoyed adult time here and there… but he and Josh were a package deal for the most part. Besides he'd finally realized that Melissa didn't really even like his son. But the rejection, again, had still stung. He wasn't sure what it was in his makeup that made women need to leave him and Josh in a cloud of dust.

"Don't even go there, friend." Gil looked at him.

"What?"

"Mandy Sue, Martha, Mary Lou—whatever—she isn't even worth your regrets."

"I don't really regret that she dumped me. We weren't right for each other."

"No kidding. You realize she didn't even like kids, right?"

"I figured that out eventually." Steve shook his head. He'd been such a clueless fool with Melissa.

"Women do seem to complicate your life, but what are you going to do? They still are sure fun to have around." Gil grinned at him. "And from what I can tell, you're enjoying having Holly around."

"I am. But it's just for a few weeks while Doc Benson is gone."

"I saw that goofy look on your face. It's about time you took another chance."

Josh came running up to them before Gil could give him any more of his lecture. *Good timing, kiddo.*

"Hi, Mr. Amaud. I found the perfect tree for Miss Holly. Come on, Dad."

Josh tugged at his hand and Steve smiled at his son's enthusiasm.

"Okay, show us the tree, son."

Gil and Steve trailed across the Christmas tree lot in the wake of the energy tornado that was his son.

That night Holly, Steve, and Josh sat in front of the newly decorated Christmas tree. They had a nice dinner of sandwiches, soup, and slices of pie from The Magnolia Cafe.

She'd actually enjoyed the evening. If someone would have told her a week ago she'd be decorating a tree for her place this year, she would have bet them a million dollars they were wrong.

"Can I go in Aunt Lucy's bedroom and watch TV? There's a movie I want to watch." Josh looked at his dad.

"That okay with you? Will he be into your things?" Steve turned to her.

"No, that's fine."

"Can I sit on the bed?"

"It's okay with me," Holly answered.

"Take your shoes off first." Steve nailed his son with an I'm-talking-to-you look.

"I will. Come on Louie. Let's go." Josh left the room, tugging off his shoes and hopping from foot to foot in the process as he went down the hallway. She heard the television come on in the bedroom.

"Wish I had a tenth of his energy." Holly twisted to face Steve on the couch, her leg tucked up to one side.

"He has boundless energy. I wish he'd share." Steve grinned that just-for-her grin he used to lower her defenses. She was sure that was what he was doing.

"You know, all day I've been thinking about kissing you again." Steve looked directly at her.

Her heart beat a little faster in an uneven rhythm. "You have?"

"Yep. But I thought I'd tell you I was going to kiss you this time. So you know. No surprises."

"Very considerate."

"I'm a considerate kind of guy." He moved over closer to her on the couch and leaned over to kiss her.

The kiss didn't come as a surprise, he'd warned her, but her reaction did. She kissed him back and threaded her hands through his hair. She wasn't sure she ever wanted him to stop. He gently cradled her face with both his hands, the warmth from them blending with the flush she felt on her cheeks.

He finally pulled back and gave a little growl. "I've been wanting that. It was better than I remembered."

"Was it?" Yes, it was. She'd admit that to herself. It was wonderful and perfect and she wanted another one. Although she could still hear the faint warning bells in the back of her mind, she chased them away, leaned over, and pulled him close again. He obliged with a deep, heated kiss, with his hands running up and down her arms.

He pulled back with another small groan. “Josh. Other room. I’d better stop while I can.”

“Um, hm.” She turned and curled against his side wanting another kiss as badly as he did, but knowing it was time to stop. For now. But, oh, how she wanted some time alone with him. To explore her feelings. To taste his kisses. To feel his hands on her. Another time. Another place. She just hoped it was soon.

Her next thoughts were filled with guilt. Then she could almost hear her friend Lynn’s voice chastising her, telling her to just enjoy the moment. She relaxed and decided to listen to Lynn even if she wasn’t even here.

CHAPTER 9

Holly stood in front of the mirror in her room and held up a simple denim skirt, a pair of black slacks, a handful of sweaters. Nothing seemed right. Steve had called the next day and said Josh was spending the night at a friend's house again and invited her to dinner. That was a problem. She had nothing to wear. She'd packed practical clothes for work. Nothing nice. Nothing sexy at all, darn it. She finally decided on a simple coral colored corduroy shirt and a heavy silver necklace with her jeans. Comfortable cowboy boots. Passable.

She pulled her hair back in a French braid with a few tendrils of hair framing her face. A touch of mascara and lipstick. She gulped in a deep breath. *Okay. Time to go.*

Her doorbell rang and she walked to the front door and opened it.

"Hi." Steve stood in the doorway dressed in jeans and a blue sweater. Her heart beat faster. He was so handsome, standing there in the glow of the Christmas lights.

"I was going to walk over."

"I thought I'd come get you and walk over with you." He paused and looked at her from the top of her head to her cowboy boots. "You look great."

"You don't look so bad yourself." Understatement. Way understatement.

She grabbed her purse and jacket and pulled the door shut behind her. Steve took her hand as they crossed over to his house. They didn't say anything on the walk. She was afraid if she spoke, her voice might squeak. Excitement and nervousness ran up and down her spine. She didn't know where the night might end up, but she knew she wanted to find out.

Steve opened the door when they got to his house. The aroma of something delicious drifted across the room.

"Smells wonderful."

"Lasagna and French bread."

"Sounds great."

"Here, let me take your coat."

Steve's voice sounded a little shaky. She wondered if he was as nervous as she was?

"Wine?"

"Yes." Maybe it would relax her.

The awkward silence continued as they sat in front of the fire.

"Dinner will be ready in about thirty minutes."

"Okay." Had she really evolved to one-word answers?

Steve let out a big sigh. "This is bad, isn't it?"

"What?" There were those one-word answers again.

"We've never been awkward talking before. What's up with tonight?"

"I don't know." There. Three words. She was proud of herself.

"I feel like a high school kid on a first date. You know the one where your dad would be right in the next room? Ready to pounce if I made a move on you."

"I've got an idea." She turned to him.

"Great."

See, she'd turned him into a one-word answerer now.

"How about you lean over and kiss me and it will break the ice."

A slow sexy grin spread across his face. "Now that's an idea I could get into." He leaned over and brushed a kiss across her lips.

"Really? That's it? Because I was expecting more. You know, in an effort to break the tension," she teased.

"You're asking for it, woman." He leaned over and kissed her thoroughly until she could barely hold a coherent thought in her head. He finally pulled back and flashed a smile. "Better?"

"Uh." Great. One word. Again. But what did he expect when he kissed her like that? It made her mind spin and her heart thump and she just wanted more. Yes, that was better. Better than better.

He stood up, took her hand and pulled her off the couch. "Why don't you come into the kitchen while I finish up dinner."

For a moment she'd thought he was going to lead her into the bedroom. The thing was, she didn't know if she was actually disappointed he hadn't. She silently chastised herself. *Get a grip*. She meekly followed him into the kitchen, unable to get control of her thoughts, and willing to just follow his lead. Besides, she really had no ability to think right now. He'd stolen that with his kiss.

Dinner was fabulous, and they relaxed and talked about anything and everything. His job. The new house he was just getting ready to dig the foundation on. Her job. His childhood dog. Her parents. Their talk wandered around like a little lost puppy and she enjoyed every moment of it.

She helped him do the dishes even though he protested he would do them himself. He poured wine and they sat on the couch in front of the fire again. The lights on the Christmas tree and the firelight tossed warm flickering golden streaks across the room. Steve shrugged off his sweater and his navy blue t-shirt stretched across his chest and his broad shoulders.

She settled against him, but he was having none of that. He pulled her into his lap. She rested her head against his shoulder, their fingers entwined and she stared at their hands in the low light. His long, strong, tanned fingers. Her short thin ones, a bit rough from her job and the constant scrubbing of her hands.

He kissed her once. Just a quick sweet kiss that hinted of so much more.

"I want to take you to bed with me." Steve's low voice rumbled against her.

She was so sure and so unsure at the same time. He nibbled at her neck sending goosebumps down her spine.

"What do you say?"

It took less than a second for her to decide. "I say, yes."

He stood up with her still in his arms and carried her to the bedroom. The room was picked up and tidy. She wondered if he always kept it this way, or if he'd cleaned it up just for her? He set her carefully near the bed.

He reached one hand behind his neck and shrugged off his t-shirt. She ran her hands along his chest.

He kissed her then. One of those mind-numbing, breath-taking-away, make-her-senseless kisses. The heat rushed through her. There was one small lamp on in the corner of the room. Just enough light to see his face.

"I'm so glad to have you here." He trailed his fingers across her lips and pushed back a lock of her hair.

"I'm glad to be here." She reached up and pulled those warm lips of his to hers.

Later, in the glow of the lamplight, he held her in his arms. Her hair fell against his shoulder like a soft silken rope, tying him in place. Unable to move, or breathe, or even think.

He drifted in and out of sleep until the daylight began to creep slowly into his room. For once he didn't want dawn to break and the day begin. He wanted to stay here in this room, with this woman sleeping in his arms. He'd no idea how she'd bewitched him in such a short time, but she had.

She stirred in his arms.

"Morning, sleepyhead."

She opened one eye and looked at him. "Really? It's morning already? Not fair." She closed her eye again.

"What time do you have to be at work?"

"Work. Darn it. What time is it?" She stirred again.

"Six."

"Ugh, I need to go. I need a shower and I need to get ready."

"How about a shower here?"

"I'm not sure I'd make it to work if I shower here." She grinned at him.

"I'll be good. I promise."

"That's what I'm afraid of."

She did grab a quick shower then stood at the mirror and reached out to wipe the moisture away and look at herself. "I look a wreck."

"You look beautiful."

"You're just saying that to see if I'll go back to bed with you." She grinned at him in the mirror.

"Hey, whatever works." He shot her a wicked grin.

She crossed into the bedroom to collect her clothes. He stood with his towel wrapped around his waist and watched her every move. Bending over to pick up her clothes. Shaking her jeans as if that would get out the wrinkles of a night of being piled on the floor. Grabbing her sweater off the chair. She finally had everything collected and slipped into her clothes.

"Here, let me get dressed and walk you back to the cottage."

"No. I'm fine. I'll just run home and change for work."

He walked her to the door and reached out to pull her into his arms once again and kissed her. Her lips kissed back eagerly. She clung to him for a moment. It took his breath away and he thought he could stand there forever. Just like this, with his mouth on hers, and her in his arms.

She finally pulled away. "I really have to go."

He nodded, unable to get any words out.

She slipped out the door. Dressed in only the towel, he stood on the porch and watched her as she walked back to the cottage. He hoped the cool air would bring him back to his senses.

CHAPTER 10

Holly's cell phone rang as she hopped on one foot, trying to wrestle her other foot into her slacks. She needed to get dressed and down some coffee. She conquered the slacks, zipping them up as she snatched the phone off the bed.

"Holls. How goes it?" Lynn's cheerful voice came through the phone.

"Do you have radar or something?"

"Yes, probably. Why? Oh, wait! Something happened with the sexy neighbor, didn't it? Did he kiss you again?"

"Um, you could say that." Holly balanced the cell phone on one shoulder while she put in an earring, then moved it to the other shoulder to put in the second earring.

"Tell me."

"We spent the night together."

"Seriously? Well, good for you."

"Now, in the light of day, I'm not sure how I feel."

"Holls, don't start second-guessing yourself."

"I can't help it."

"Yes, you can. Just stop it. Tell yourself I ordered you to stop. Do whatever it takes. Live in the moment."

"I just met him a week or so ago. What am I doing?"

"I told you. You don't always get to pick when someone wonderful will come into your life. It happens. Not always as you planned. Not always when it's convenient."

"I know."

"Then what's the problem?"

"Besides the fact I live halfway across the country? Besides the fact my job is miles away too? Besides the fact I've only known him for a week or so? You mean besides those problems?" Holly sat on the bed and tugged on a shoe.

"Yes, besides those."

She could hear the smile she knew was plastered across Lynn's face.

"And besides the fact my best friend is way far away in the Midwest?"

"Ah, but we have cell phones and video chat."

"We do have that."

"You like him a lot, don't you? You must or this would never have happened."

"I do like him. Lots. It's just very confusing right now."

"Well, promise me one thing."

"What's that?"

"Don't overthink this like you usually overthink everything."

Her best friend knew her so well. "I'll try not to."

"Good. I gotta run. Oh, and I sent you something, did you get it yet?"

"No. You didn't need to send me something."

"I wasn't sure I should send it…" Lynn paused. "Just open it, Holls. I hope I did the right thing."

"Now you're being mysterious."

"I… Anyway, open it. Is it okay to say Merry Christmas to you now that you aren't all Scrooged out?"

Holly smiled. "Yes, it's fine."

"Then, Merry Christmas. Call me if you need to talk."

"Okay. I will. Thanks for calling."

"Remember. No overthinking."

She heard Lynn end the call. She tugged on her other shoe and went to look in the mirror. Her cheeks were flushed and her eyes were a mix of tired and excited if that were even possible. She pulled her hair back in a loose braid and grabbed her things. It was going to be a long day of work with as little sleep as she had gotten last night.

The day didn't prove her wrong. She was so tired when the last lady left with her collie with the cut paw. She sighed and tilted her head from one side to the other, trying to work out the kink in her neck. Probably from sleeping on Steve's arm most of the night.

Luckily she'd been way too busy today to overthink anything about last night. Tonight she planned on soaking in the tub for a good long time with a glass of wine, candlelight, and her ereader.

Steve hadn't called all day, and she didn't know whether she was glad about that or upset. But he'd probably been busy all day, too. She was so unsure about so much.

Holly drove home and pulled into the driveway, noticing Steve's house was completely dark except for the Christmas lights on the front bushes. She slowly got out of the car and walked to the front steps of the cottage. There, by the front door, was a package. It looked to be flowers wrapped in paper. She carried it inside, dropped her purse and keys on the table by the door and carried the package to the kitchen. She carefully pulled back the paper and saw a vase of fresh holly covered in red berries. A red ribbon was tied around the vase. She read the attached card.

Had a wonderful time last night. Thought of you all day. Taking Josh to the movies tonight, but hope to see you tomorrow night for Christmas Eve. I don't know your favorite flower. Must find out. Steve.

So, he had thought of her today. She placed the vase of holly in the center of the kitchen table. The cottage was getting more and more Christmasy as her stay wore on, and it didn't bother her, she realized. She'd always loved Christmas, a season filled with friends and family. Last year had been so horrible, with none of that. She'd thought that what she needed this year was to hide out from the holidays. But it no longer felt right to hide. She crossed into the family room and plugged in the Christmas tree lights. The low glow from the lights made the room seem magical. This week had been magical. She didn't know where things were headed. She only had about another week left here, but she was no longer afraid of the holidays. If that were the only good thing to happen this holiday season, she'd take that. But then there was Steve. And Josh. And Louie. So much had changed in such a short time.

Christmas Eve with Steve and Josh sounded like just the way she'd like to spend Christmas. She smiled to herself, actually pleased she had holiday plans now. Eager to see Steve again. She'd bought a model kit for Josh and a book on famous architecturally interesting houses for Steve. She'd even gotten a bone from the butcher for Louie. She'd planned to drop the gifts off sometime during Christmas, but now she'd have them for Christmas Eve.

She found herself humming a Christmas carol under her breath as she drew her bath and lit some candles. She slipped into the hot water and felt the most relaxed she had in days. Weeks. Well, since last night at Steve's in front of the fire anyway. She flipped open her ereader and started reading a new novel. She hadn't read all year long either. She'd been afraid of slowing down and relaxing. She was soon sucked into the mystery, pausing every so often to run more hot water into the tub.

She finally climbed out of the tub and toweled off. The fabric of the towel rubbed across her tender skin. The skin that yearned for Steve's warm hands to be trailing all over her body again. She shook her head. This trip to Comfort Crossing sure wasn't turning out like she'd planned.

CHAPTER 11

Holly had a half day in the clinic on Christmas Eve. They weren't very busy but had a couple of minor emergencies to handle. Steve had called and said they'd walk over about six and pick her up for Christmas Eve at his house. She was looking forward to it and was glad she'd picked up the small gifts for them this week.

Her cell phone rang and she saw it was Steve again.

"Hi, Steve."

"Holly. Good, you're still there. It's Louie. He was hit by a car. We're on our way."

"Oh. I'm so sorry. I'll be here."

Within five minutes Steve came in carrying Louie, wrapped in a bloody blanket. Josh trailed behind, crying. "It's all my fault. I wasn't looking when I crossed the street. Louie was following me. It's all my fault."

"Come back to the examining room. Let me look at him."

Steve set Louie on the exam table and pulled Josh over to sit in a chair. "Let her do her job, Josh."

Holly looked at Louie's injuries. They were serious. Very serious. It was happening again. Just like last year. Just like her Tucker. The universe was taunting her, showing what happened when she tried to move forward with her life.

She forced herself to breathe steadily, to push back the thoughts of last year. "I'm going to have to operate." Holly looked at Steve.

"Is he going to be okay? Promise?" Josh pleaded with her.

"I'm going to try my best, Josh. I can't promise anything though. I'm sorry. He's really hurt."

She felt she was in a dream, a repeat of last year. Spending Christmas Eve trying to save an animal she loved, one year later from the night she lost her husband and her dog, Tucker. Only this year, she wanted the outcome to be better. She wanted Louie to live. She needed him to live. Her heart tightened in her chest.

This is what happens when you let your guard down. Life sneaks up and smacks you back into place.

She gritted her teeth against the wave of memories trying to overwhelm her. She'd give anything for any vet in the whole wide world to be the one working on Louie. But there were no other vets around for miles and miles. It was all up to her.

She spent hours working on Louie, but she still wasn't sure he was going to make it. She went out to the waiting room where Steve and Josh were waiting for news.

"Is he okay?" Josh jumped up, ran up to her, and threw his arms around her waist.

"I'm not sure. He made it through surgery but he's not out of the woods yet."

"You have to save him, Miss Holly. You have to."

"I'm trying, Josh." She wouldn't lie to the boy. Wouldn't promise that Louie would make it. She couldn't.

Steve slowly pushed himself out of the chair and came to put his arm around Josh. "Josh, she's doing her best."

Holly was deathly afraid her best wouldn't be good enough, yet again. Steve reached out to touch her shoulder, and she flinched. His eyes questioned her, but he didn't say anything in front of Josh.

"I'm going to go check on Louie again. I'll stay with him. Why don't you two both go home?"

"I'm not leaving." Josh stood there defiantly.

"Okay, we'll stay awhile longer, bud." Steve gave his son an encouraging nod.

"I'll be in the back. I'll come out soon and let you know how he's doing."

They stayed that way for hours. She'd come out and say there was no change with Louie. Josh would insist on staying. Repeat. Finally, about midnight, when she went to the waiting room, Josh was sound asleep.

"There is no change. I'm sorry. Why don't you bring him home?" Holly nodded towards Josh.

Steve raked his hands through his hair. He looked tired. His face was creased and set with pain. For Josh. For his son's dog. He stood up and tried to put his arms around her.

She panicked and stepped back, away from the embrace. She chastised herself for believing things could be different. That she could care again and not get hurt. "Don't."

"Don't what? Don't hold you? Don't care

about you?" His voice was low and held a hint of accusation.

"I just can't. I can't do this again." Her pulse pounded in her ears, her heart tightened in her chest.

"Do what? Care about an animal again and risk the loss? Or are you talking about caring about me, too?" His eyes pierced through the distance between them.

"Steve, I…" Her heart beat in a riotous rhythm and she fought to keep control. "I can't do this, not again. I'll try to save Louie. I hope I can this time. But I was wrong. It's too soon for me. I'm sorry."

Steve looked at her and she watched as his eyes turned a dark, smoldering shade of brown. His face hardened. He nodded. "Call if there is any change." His words were icy cold. He crossed the waiting room, scooped up his son and disappeared into the night. She could see the Christmas lights on Main Street mocking her. *See what happens when you care?*

She spent the night in the clinic, falling asleep in a chair beside Louie's kennel sometime in the early morning. When she awoke, she could see Louie was awake and looking at her. "Hey, boy. Good morning. How you feeling?" She kept her voice low and soothing.

A quick exam proved to her that he was doing so much better. It never ceased to amaze her how an animal could pull through when she least expected it. Well, her Tucker hadn't. But, thank goodness, Louie was going to be all right. She could feel it. He'd turned that corner.

The vet tech, Cindy, called and said she'd heard about Louie, and how was he doing? After she heard that Louie was doing better, she offered to come in and watch Louie while Holly went home and got some sleep. That sounded good to Holly. She was exhausted. Not only from being up most of the night for the last two nights, but she was emotionally drained. She'd jumped into a relationship with Steve—and Josh—and Louie, for that matter. The universe had laughed at her and thrown her into an almost repeat of last year. A deep loneliness crept over her, smothering her, making her want to run away. Far away. But it seemed like wherever she ran, there was no escaping.

As much as she wanted to avoid him, she had to call Steve and tell him Louie would be okay.

She dialed his number, and he picked up on the first ring.

"Louie is doing better. He's going to make it."

"Josh, Miss Holly says Louie's doing better. He's going to be okay."

Holly could hear his conversation with Josh and Josh's cheering in the background. She could almost picture the small boy's jig of happiness. She smiled a small weak smile.

"Thanks for letting us know." Steve's voice still held that frigid edge.

She didn't blame him. She'd slept with him then pushed him away the next day. But she just couldn't do it again. She couldn't. Dave had only been gone a year. It was too soon.

She heard him click off his phone before she could even say "you're welcome."

Within an hour she was walking up her front steps, wanting nothing more than to climb into bed and sleep away the day. There on the front porch was a package. Probably the one Lynn said she'd sent.

She dropped it on the couch, too tired to open it. After a hot shower, she crawled into bed. It was late afternoon when she woke up. She'd better get moving and get back to the clinic and check on Louie.

After some coffee.

She climbed out of bed and headed for the kitchen, noticing the package on the couch. She scooped it up and carried it to the kitchen. She made the coffee and sat down to open the package while the coffee was brewing.

She unwrapped the brown mailing paper and saw a note in Lynn's handwriting taped on the package wrapped in Christmas paper. She opened the note. All it said was *I hope I did the right thing. Found this while cleaning out that messy storage room at work.*

She unwrapped the crinkled Christmas paper and pulled off the lid to the box. She caught her breath when she saw a note from Dave resting inside the box.

I love you, hon. I believe in you. I love how you let go of fear and follow your dreams.

Always and forever,

Dave

She pulled back the tissue paper to find a silver ornament of a soaring eagle.

Tears flooded her eyes now and rolled down in

hot tracks across her cheeks. Dave. He'd always known how to say the right thing at the right time. He must have bought this last year before the accident and hidden it in the storage room at work. He'd always claimed she found all his hiding places. But not last year. She ran her finger over the shiny silver of the ornament. The bird soaring free.

She took it as a sign. A sign from Dave. He'd always been there for her, and he was again. Just when she needed him. Dave was right. She needed to get over her fears. She needed to start living again even if it meant getting hurt. She'd made such a mess of things with Steve.

That ended now. She grabbed some coffee, placed the ornament carefully on her Christmas tree, and hurried to get ready to go to the clinic and check on Louie. Then she'd find Steve.

Steve saw Holly pull up and park in front of the clinic. He'd brought Josh over to see Louie. The vet tech had let Josh sit in the back for a bit with the dog. He'd been glad to see Cindy at the clinic instead of Holly. He hadn't wanted to face Holly. He'd clung to the false hope he'd make it through the rest of her temporary stay here in Comfort Crossing without ever seeing her again.

But all those hopes of avoiding her just flew out the window he was looking out right now. With each step she took closer to the front door, he could feel his heart hardening more. He was finished with women rejecting him, rejecting Josh. Finished. He'd learned his lesson well this time.

Her rejection of him stung, he admitted that. He'd fallen for her. Fallen hard, after all these years of going it alone. But he could take the rejection and move on. He knew he could do that. *Couldn't he?*

But, by rejecting him, she'd rejected Josh, too. The boy was nuts about her. He couldn't forgive that. He had to protect his son. His son had had too many losses in his young life. His mother left, his grandmother died, even his aunt had moved away. Now he was going to lose Holly, too. He should have protected his son better than this. What had he been thinking?

Holly pushed through the door. "Steve."

He just nodded at her and went and slid into one of the hard, uncomfortable, waiting room chairs. *You'd think Doc Benson could have better chairs for the room.*

"I wanted to talk to you, but let me go check on Louie first."

"Be nice to Josh."

Her eyes widen. "Of course I will."

He ignored her answer and picked up a magazine.

She came back about five minutes later. "Louie is doing well. I think you can take him home tomorrow. You'll have to keep him quiet, but he's doing better than I even had hoped for."

He nodded at her again. Unwilling to speak. Oh, he was grateful she'd saved Louie. He'd always be grateful for that. But it ended there. A man could only take so much rejection.

"Steve, can we talk?"

"There's not much left to say, is there?"

"I'm sorry."

"No need to be. Just a misunderstanding on my part. I read more into us than there was."

"It's not that. I was afraid. It was all beginning to feel so much like last year. The loss. Working on Louie, just like I had on Tucker last year. I was so afraid I wouldn't be able to save Louie, either. There was so much loss in my life last year."

"So, instead you just toss me away. Wouldn't that have been a better decision to make before the other night?"

"I was scared. I admit. But, I got this gift from Dave… it was like he was giving me his blessing or something. Urging me to not let fear stop me, to go after my dreams. Steve, I want to try. I do. I want to see where things go with us." Her eyes were full of hope.

He ignored them. *Really he did.*

He couldn't afford to get involved with someone who didn't know what they wanted from one day to the next. Who might hurt Josh, and if he were being honest, hurt him again. He was so tired of women leaving him.

"That's not going to work for me." He wasn't going to waver. He'd made up his mind.

"What do you mean? Don't you want to see where this goes with us? Can't you understand I was just… scared?"

The look in her eyes almost made him change his mind, but then he remembered his son. All that he'd lost. "Holly, I can't. I can't take the chance with Josh. It would be easier if you just leave when you're finished here at Doc Benson's. I can't risk you changing your mind again. Ping-ponging back and forth while you figure out what you want from life. Josh can't take another woman he adores leaving him. His mother left him, he lost my mom, his aunt moved away. That's way too much loss for a boy his age. I know you've had your losses, but so have we. You need to stay away from Josh, from us. Just go back home."

He felt himself torn in half, giving his speech on protecting Josh. He wanted Holly. Wanted to take a chance, just like she'd finally decided to do. But he couldn't risk Josh. Risk him being left again. He didn't trust that Holly wouldn't pull away again. Best to end it now before Josh became even more attached. No more outings. No more inviting her over. He'd do anything for his son. Anything. *Even give up a chance with Holly.*

A lone tear trailed down Holly's cheek. She didn't even bother to hide it from him. It tore at him to see her hurt, but he had to. Had to protect Josh.

She slowly turned and headed back to check on Louie. He sat down in the lonely waiting room and stared out the window.

If he were being totally honest with himself —which he wasn't going to be— he was just as afraid of getting hurt himself as he was of Josh getting hurt. He was a coward. Afraid to risk rejection and loss. Even for a shot at love.

So he went back to believing he was only doing this for Josh. It was a fantasy that allowed him to not face his own fears.

CHAPTER 12

Steve looked up to see Gil come through the door to Doc Benson's clinic. His friend crossed the waiting room in long strides as Steve rose up to greet him.

"I heard about Louie. Thought I'd come by and check on him and you guys. How's he doing? How's Josh?"

"Louie is doing better. He's got a long recovery ahead of him, but he's going to make it."

Steve saw relief cross his friend's face.

"That is great news."

Steve nodded.

Gil looked at him closely for a moment. "So, what's up? You don't look all that happy about it."

"No, I'm so glad Louie is going to be okay."

"But?"

His friend knew him too well. Steve sighed. "It's a long story but Holly said she didn't want to see me anymore. She lost her husband in an accident last Christmas. Killed instantly. Her dog was with him in the car, and she worked on him, but couldn't save him. She lost them both. This thing with Louie brought it all crashing back on her."

"Man, that's tough on her. I can see why she backed away. Just give her some time."

"That's the thing. By this morning she *had* changed her mind. Now she wants to keep trying, see where we are—*were*—headed."

"She was probably just shaken up last night, but then had time to think it through."

Gil had more compassion for Holly than he'd shown her. Steve rolled his shoulders, trying to loosen the tension. "Well, I told her no. I can't take a chance. Josh is already crazy about her. If she changes her mind again… I don't want him to get hurt."

"Or you don't want to take a chance and you get hurt again?"

Gil always asked the tough questions. Always.

Steve went and stared out the window. "I don't know. I don't want Josh to get hurt, but I don't really want to get closer to Holly, only to have her change her mind. Again."

"For Pete's sake, Steve. Even I can realize how hard last night had to have been for Holly—and my sister says I'm a clueless male. It had to have been horrible for Holly after what happened to her last Christmas. It was probably a knee-jerk reaction. She was probably exhausted. Why can't you give her a chance?"

"I just don't think I can."

"Ah, then you're a bigger fool than I thought possible. You sometimes have to take big risks for love. Don't be a jerk. Tell her how you feel. Think about it."

Steve turned to his friend. He nodded, but he still wasn't sure he was strong enough to take the chance.

Gil smiled. "Well, I better go, before my sister comes looking for me. Supposed to be having Christmas dinner with her and the boys. Glad Louie is doing okay." His friend crossed to the door then turned and glanced back. "Come on, old man. You can do it. Take a chance." Then he was gone.

Holly went to her office and swiped away the tears. She hadn't blamed Steve. She understood exactly where he was coming from. She'd destroyed his trust in her when she pushed him away. Now he didn't want to take a chance on her. One of the qualities she admired about him, his loyalty to his son, was exactly what was going to keep them apart. Steve didn't trust that she wouldn't change her mind again. She wasn't sure she'd trust herself either if she were him.

She sank down in the chair and gave herself a few minutes to pull herself together. She didn't want Josh to see her looking like this. Cindy had left two messages on her desk from people who had called, checking on Louie. Small towns. Everyone knew about everything. Even a small boy's dog. She liked that about Comfort Crossing. She was going to miss this town.

She got her emotions under control and stood up to go check on Louie.

"Where's Josh?" Holly entered the room where they were keeping Louie. Cindy looked up from where she was doing some bookwork at the desk. "Josh went out to join you guys in the waiting room."

"When?"

"Five minutes or so?"

"Hm. Must have missed him. I'll go talk to him about Louie."

Holly hurried back to the waiting room to find Steve alone in the waiting room. "Where's Josh?"

"I thought he was in the back with Cindy." Steve looked up at her questioningly.

"Cindy said he came out to the waiting room."

Steve levered himself out of the chair and stood up. He called down the hall. "Josh? Where are you, bud?"

Steve checked the bathroom while Holly checked the storeroom.

"I can't find him." The beginning of panic was clearly etched on Steve's face.

"Where would he go?" Holly had no clue why Josh would leave and had no idea where he'd go.

"I don't know. It doesn't make any sense."

"I'll help you look for him."

Steve glanced at her and for a moment she thought he would turn down her help, but he nodded yes.

Holly went and asked Cindy to stay, but to call if Josh showed up. She grabbed her coat and they headed out the door.

"Where should we start?" Holly followed Steve out the door.

"I need to think. I'm not sure. We can check my office, he knows where I hide the key."

They walked to his office, but the door was locked and the key still in its hiding place. Steve opened the door and looked around anyway, calling for his son. She could hear the panic firmly entrenched in his voice now.

"We'll find him." She touched his arm, willing him strength.

"Why would he run away? I don't understand." The pain cracked through Steve's voice.

His pain tore at her. She was beginning to feel the panic creep up on her too, but she fought it away. She had to remain calm for Steve. It was the least she could do.

Steve stood and looked up and down the street, paralyzed.

"Let's keep looking. How about the park?"

"Good idea. He used to always hang out by that log cabin playhouse at the edge of the park." Steve hurried down Main Street with long strides, heading towards the park. Holly had to almost run to keep up with him. They crossed into the park and past the gazebo.

"Josh?" Steve called out his son name. "Josh, answer me. Please."

"I'm here, Dad."

Holly heard the small voice and her heart swelled with relief. The boy came out of the log cabin playhouse, tears running down his face.

"Josh!" Steve swept his son up in his arms and held him close. The boy clung to his father and buried his face in Steve's shoulder.

Hot tears filled Holly's eyes. Josh was safe. They'd found him. She wanted to rush up and snatch him into her arms and hold him, but Steve had made it clear he wanted no part of her, for him or for Josh. He'd made it clear she was to stay away. She didn't even blame him. She'd really messed up. Her heart went from joyful pounding at finding the boy, to sinking with the knowledge of all she had ruined.

"Why did you leave, Josh?" Steve questioned his son.

"It's all my fault."

"What is, son?" Steve put Josh down on the ground and knelt beside him.

"Louie, that's my fault. He was just following me and he got hurt. Then you won't like Miss Holly because of me." The boy sniffed.

"Josh, nothing is your fault." Steve wrapped his arms around Josh, holding him tight. He then released the boy and put a hand on each of the boy's small shoulders. "Did you listen to Miss Holly and I talking?"

"Yes, I know I'm not supposed to. But I heard you arguing."

"I'm sorry you heard all that."

"But, Dad, why won't you like Miss Holly? I like her. She's not going to leave us, are you Miss Holly?"

The boy's bright blue eyes looked up at her. No, she couldn't ever imagine leaving them. He had her heart hopelessly wrapped around his finger.

She knew the answer Steve wanted her to give. That she was leaving as soon as her job was over and Doc Benson came back. But she couldn't say the words. She shot a pleading look at Steve and hoped he'd forgive her because she was going to tell the truth. Tell what was in her heart.

"No, I don't believe I could leave you, Josh. When we couldn't find you? I felt like my heart was breaking. I could barely breathe. I couldn't imagine my life without you… or without your father."

There. She'd said it. Out loud.

She just hoped that was good enough for Steve. That he'd realize just how much she cared, not only about him, but for Josh. Cared with her whole heart. She wasn't going to let herself get scared away again.

"Josh, I tried to hide away from people for a long time. It's complicated, but I was hurt and it was easier to just not get close to people, to care about them. But, you know? You came bursting into my life, and I'm really glad. I care about both you and your father. And Louie, of course."

"I know you do. I could tell. I'm old enough to figure that out." Josh puffed up his chest and stood tall. "See, Dad. Now you tell her you can like her. Please, Dad. Please." The boy turned those bright blue eyes on his father. *Ha, see if he did a better job resisting Josh than she had.*

Steve was quiet for a moment. She was sure he was going to turn to her with those brittle brown eyes filled with anger. She hadn't followed his wishes, the ones where he wanted her out of their lives to protect his son.

He looked at her then, for a long, long moment, searching her face. She could almost see the thoughts, doubts, hopes, and questions whirling around his mind.

Josh moved over to her and took her hand, turning back to look at his father.

Steve slowly stood up, raked his hands through his hair, and gave a big sigh. He slowly shook his head back and forth. Then he grinned that slow, sexy smile of his. Her heart swelled and filled with hope. Maybe it wasn't too late.

Then a serious look swept over his face. "I might have been a bit hasty in not accepting your apology. Oh, heck. I was a fool. Last night must have been such a nightmare for you. I should have been more understanding of how scared you were. You've probably already figured out that I'm not too good with relationships." He stood up and slowly crossed the distance between them and took her hand.

"Well, if Miss Holly is willing to like me, I think I'd be willing to like her right back."

Her heart began to sing. Steve looked at her, his eyes questioning her.

"I'm willing to like you." She looked up at him and felt a smile sweep across her face, then an outright grin.

"Good. It's settled." He leaned down and brushed a light kiss on her lips. A kiss filled with hope for the future.

"Yuck, Dad. You don't have to kiss her, do you?"

"I'm afraid I do, son."

With that he pulled her into a hug and brushed one more quick kiss across her lips. Josh danced back and forth beside them. “Okay, that’s enough, already. Let’s go back and see Louie. I can’t wait to tell him the news.”

Dear Reader,

Did you miss the start of this series? Click here to get the first book for free now! The Shop on Main - Book One.
Or continue on to read another heartwarming holiday story, A Christmas Scarf.

See all my books at my website.

COMFORT CROSSING ~ A NOVELLA

The Christmas Scarf

KAY CORRELL

Published by Rose Quartz Press

090516

This book is dedicated to my mother and my grandmothers who made each and every Christmas a magical time of year.

CHAPTER 1

Missy Sherwood glanced around at the bare walls and empty room. The late afternoon light filtered in through the battered blinds on the small window. She'd always planned to replace them but never had found the time or money to do so. Probably just as well since she'd only be leaving them behind now.

She slowly left the room, closing the door behind her. She crossed the cramped space that served as a kitchen and sitting room and dropped her apartment key on the counter. It was best that her two roommates were at work now. She didn't really want a fancy goodbye, or even words of encouragement.

She'd tried to take Nashville by storm, wanting to be a country singer along with every third person in the city. All the singers-slash-waiters or singers-slash-receptionists.

Now the company where she worked as a receptionist had closed, so she'd lost that job and couldn't remember the last time she'd even had a backup singing gig in spite of constantly going to auditions. She'd had high hopes of getting hired as a backup singer to Keith Harper after getting a second call back, but nothing. She'd promised herself she would give herself until the end of this year to make it, if not, she would call it quits and find another way to make a living.

The Christmas lights blinked on a pathetic but free tree in the corner. She placed two small presents beneath the tree for her roommates.

She tugged a hat on her short, unruly curls and with one last look around the apartment, she turned and headed out the door, pulling it firmly closed behind her. She walked the three blocks it took to get to the parking garage, hauling a suitcase with a large tote bag balanced on top and her guitar in her other hand. The garage had been the closest parking space she could afford by her apartment. Christmas decorations dotted the store windows as she walked past. Music spilled out on the street when a man hurried out of a liquor store. She walked into the parking garage and struggled up the two flights of stairs to her spot. At least she wouldn't have to wrestle her way up and down these stairs anymore.

She set her guitar in the back seat of the car. With a tug and a push, she leveraged the heavy suitcase into the trunk and dropped the tote bag on top of it. The slam of the trunk echoed through the garage, closing on the end of her non-existent career, the end of her dreams.

She had nowhere else to go but home.

Missy sat in her car on the street in front of her mother's house. She was sure this was the house though she hadn't ever been there before. Her mother and her new husband had moved in a few years back. If only they'd stayed in the house she'd grown up in, where she felt at least a bit like she belonged. At that house she would have just walked in the door, calling out for her mother. But at this house, she was almost a stranger. She'd only met her mother's new husband a handful of times, at the wedding, and a couple of times when they'd come through Nashville on one of their many trips.

Now she was just going to show up on their doorstep? What was she thinking?

But what choices did she have? Out of work. Barely enough savings to survive until she found some kind of work. Any kind of work. Her things were in the basement storage at her apartment—her former apartment—and she'd assured her roommates she'd be back for them soon. She couldn't face coming home to Comfort Crossing with her belongings crammed into her car, announcing her defeat. She needed a few weeks to adjust to everything.

She swung open the car door and headed for the front porch. Her mother, as usual, had decorated the house to within an inch of its life. It had embarrassed her as a young girl growing up, but now it made her smile, a touch of familiarity in her life. She climbed the porch steps and rang the doorbell.

The door swung wide. "Missy." Her mother smothered her in a hug and covered her with flour at the same time from the bag she held in her hand. "Oh, I'm sorry. Look at the mess. I was baking. Guess there's a rip in the flour sack. Come in, come in. Why didn't you call? No, never mind, I'm just so glad to see you."

Her mother bustled her inside as Missy let her

mother's words wash over her. It was always a stream of sentences with her mother.

"Hi, Mom. Thought I'd come home for Christmas and surprise you."

A look of concern flashed across her mother's eyes, but was quickly hidden behind her smile. "Well, come in and sit in the kitchen. I have a batch of cookies about to come out of the oven."

"Oatmeal?" Missy could only hope for her favorite.

"Oatmeal it is. I was going to mail off a batch to you later today. But here you are."

Missy followed her mother to the back of the house and sat down in a large kitchen with high white cabinets, stainless appliances, and the largest stovetop she'd ever seen. Her mother must be in heaven. She loved spending time in the kitchen. Light flowed in the big windows and a breakfast nook was tucked over near the side.

"Mom, your kitchen is beautiful."

"It is, isn't it? I tell you, Dwayne spoils me. He had the whole kitchen redone and let me pick out everything. We had a formal living room, but who needs that? We knocked down the wall between the living room and kitchen and made the kitchen bigger." Her mother pulled a baking sheet of cookies from one of the double ovens. "I guess they finally decided to give you some time off for the holidays? I know you always say it's a busy time of the year and hard to get away. It will be so nice to have you here this year, though. So nice. It's been so long since you've been home for the holidays. Cookie?"

She'd missed her mother's rambles. And her cookies. Missy decided it wasn't really a good time to go into the fact she was homeless and jobless. She reached over and snagged an oatmeal cookie. Nothing like comfort food to chase away a person's problems.

The back door swung open and Dwayne entered with his arms full of packages. "I think I got everything you need for baking your cookies for the tree lighting ceremony." Dwayne hip checked the door closed behind him, then saw Missy sitting at the island in the kitchen.

"Missy. Great to see you." Dwayne set the sacks on the counter.

"Thanks, good to see you, too."

Missy caught a quick look flash between Dwayne and her mother and that hint of concern popped up in her mother's eyes again.

"Missy has come home for the holidays." Her mother rolled a bit of cookie into a ball and plopped it onto the baking sheet.

"You don't say. Well, that's nice." There was that look between Dwayne and her mother again.

"I really should have called first..." Missy shifted back on the counter stool.

"No, of course not, dear." Her mother plopped another cookie on the baking sheet.

"Well, I'll let you two catch up. I'm going to head back to the Gazette. Got to get the weekly paper all put to bed." Dwayne headed out the back door.

"He's been the editor at the paper for like a million years, hasn't he?"

"Twenty or so. Along with running an insurance business, but he's retired from that and just works at the paper now."

"Mom, is everything okay? You've got that look..."

"What look?"

"That look that says something is wrong and you're trying to fix it for everyone."

Her mother washed her hands and sat down on the stool beside Missy. "Well, it's just that Dwayne's two daughters and their husbands are coming for Christmas. They each have two kids. We only have three bedrooms. But we'll make it work."

"I should have called. I'm sorry."

Her mother leaned over and wrapped her in a hug. "Don't be silly. You're always welcome here. I'll sort it out. The more the merrier."

"Thanks, Mom."

But even at home in Comfort Crossing, the town she grew up in, she felt out of place.

Missy headed over to Main Street with no real purpose in mind. She loved that she could walk from her mother's new home to Main Street. She could walk to almost any place she wanted to in Comfort Crossing. She'd forgotten how nice that was. It was a bit chilly this time of year, with a nip to the air. She pulled her jacket closed to keep out the wind. Her hometown was an interesting mix of weather. A person would be just as likely to be wearing jeans and a t-shirt this time of year as they were to be bundled up in jackets.

She crossed down the side street and came out on Main. Decorations and lights were strung across the street. Each business had elaborate decorations in their windows in preparation for the window decorating contest the town held each year. She'd forgotten about that. There was a lot she'd forgotten about her hometown in her years away.

Magnolia Cafe was right across the street and she decided to pop in and see if her cousin still worked there. She hadn't seen Becky Lee in years. Missy pushed through the door of the cafe and the smell of cinnamon twirled around her, whisking her back in time, filling her with memories. Christmas music drifted through the restaurant. Now this felt like home. She'd spent so many hours here, with friends or just sitting and chatting with Becky Lee as she worked.

"Missy Sherwood, don't you even give your cousin a heads up when you're coming to town?" Becky Lee set down a tray of dishes and hurried over and smothered her with a hug. "You are a sight for sore eyes. I've missed you, Cuz."

"I've missed you too, Bec."

"You come home for the holidays? You haven't been here for Christmas in forever. Aunt Clara said you never get time off this time of year. I guess the nightclubs and bars are busy during the holidays, huh?"

"Well, I, uh… I have the time this year."

"Good for you for making it a priority." Becky Lee gave Missy one more hug. "I gotta get back to work. Grab a table by the window. Just a couple of tables left over from the lunch crowd and I'll be able to sit for a bit."

Missy shrugged off her jacket and sat at a table by the window looking out on Main Street. Shoppers hustled by, laden with packages. Which reminded her she still needed to find a gift for her mother and Dwayne. An inexpensive gift.

Becky Lee swung by the table. "Pecan pie and coffee? You haven't gone all diet-y on me, have you?"

"Pecan pie for sure. No one makes pecan pie like Magnolia Cafe."

Becky dropped off the pie and coffee at the table. "Be finished in a sec."

Missy took a bite of the pie, savoring it. She'd missed this pie and she'd missed her cousin. She'd avoided coming home for the holidays for too long. Oh, she knew why she hadn't come home. Everyone always asked about her music. Where she was playing now. Thinking she had some glamorous life in Nashville, playing in trendy bars and nightclubs. She hadn't bothered to mention to anyone that her main income was a series of low paying clerical jobs and waitressing.

Becky Lee came over and plopped into the seat across from Missy. "Going to have a cup of coffee with you before I start in on the after-lunch chores. So, catch me up on your life."

"Not much to say, really."

Becky Lee cocked her head to one side. "You okay?"

"Sure, I'm fine. Just a bit tired from the drive here, I guess."

"So, how did you like your mom's kitchen? Pretty great, isn't it?"

"It is. Dwayne sure knows how to make Mom happy, give her a nice kitchen to bake in. I bet she's barely had that oven off since the kitchen was finished."

"She's probably busy making cookies for the tree lighting ceremony, isn't she? She always helps out with that."

"She is. She was making oatmeal cookies when I was there and was headed into making chocolate chip."

"That's my Aunt Clara. I think I must have gotten my baking genes from her. I sure didn't get them from my mom."

Missy glanced out the window just then and saw him. Shawn Poole.

Becky Lee must have seen the surprise on her face because she looked out the window to see what Missy was staring at. "Ah, Shawn."

Missy cleared her throat. "What's he up to these days?"

"He works with his dad at the landscape business. They've got some big contracts now with the school and two of the plantations right out of town. Their company does landscaping and lawn care now. They still have the Christmas tree lot every year, too."

"He always did like working outside with his dad."

Just then a little boy came running up to Shawn and he scooped him up in his arms. The little boy smothered him with kisses.

Becky Lee looked over at Missy then back out on the street to Shawn. "That's his son."

Missy caught her breath. His son. Shawn had a son.

"He married Belinda Rider."

Her thoughts were a riotous mess of memories and feelings. "Really? Belinda? Wasn't she a year behind me in school?"

"I think so. Anyway, they started dating after you left. Got married about four years ago. Their son is about three now, I think."

"Wow. Somehow I just never pictured Shawn as the settling-down-having-a-kid type."

"Well, he is now. They seem really happy."

Good for Shawn. He was happy now. *That was just great. Great.*

Of course, he'd always said he'd be happy in Nashville with her. Until he said he wasn't going with her the night before they were set to leave.

"You okay?" Becky Lee set down her coffee and reached across the table to touch Missy's hand.

"I'm just… surprised. A lot has changed here, hasn't it?"

"Some things change here, some things stay the same. Like your love for our pecan pie." Becky Lee smiled and nodded toward the empty pie plate.

"That won't ever change. Love that pie."

"So, I bet your mom was glad to see you."

"She was, though I guess I should have called first. She's going to have a houseful of Dwayne's family for Christmas."

"Well, then you should stay with me." Becky Lee's eyes lit up. "I'd love to have someone for the holidays. Heck, I'm just around the corner from your mom's place. You can go over there for whatever festivities you want to but have an actual room and bed at my place. What do you say?"

"I say yes. That would be great. Mom will be

relieved to have a solution to the whole how-do-I-fit-everyone-in problem."

"The key is under the flowerpot by the front door. When I even remember to lock the door."

"That will work out great, thank you."

"Well, I better get back to work." Becky Lee stood up. "You go over there and unpack anytime. You know where the guest bedroom is. I'm working the dinner shift, too, but I should be home around nine thirty or so."

"Perfect. I'll see you tonight."

CHAPTER 2

Missy told her mother about her plans to stay at Becky Lee's and noticed the relief that flashed across her mother's face. Her mother was the ultimate hostess, but only had so much space for a holiday crowd of visitors.

She moved her car from in front of her mother's house to park by Becky Lee's cute little cottage. She got out of the car and popped the trunk.

"Missy, is that you?"

She looked up to see Dylan Rivers loping across the street to her. He looked the same. Dark brown hair worn just a tad too long. The ever-present hint of a day old beard. Broad shoulders, long legs, and an easy stride.

"Hey, I didn't know you were in town." Dylan

swooped her up into a hug. "I haven't seen you in years. I hear things are going great for you in Nashville. I expect to hear you on the radio any day now."

This was exactly why she hadn't come home in so many years.

"Dylan, hi. It's great to see you."

"You staying at Becky Lee's?" Dylan nodded towards the cottage.

"I am. Mom's got a houseful of Dwayne's family coming for the holidays."

"Let me help you haul your things in." Dylan reached into the trunk and grabbed the suitcase and tote bag.

Missy grabbed the guitar and they headed into the cottage. She bent down to get the key from under the flowerpot but laughed when Dylan just turned the knob and the door swung open.

"Gotta love this town. Been a long time since I've been somewhere that you don't lock your doors."

"Part of our charm." Dylan stood back holding the door for Missy to cross inside in front of him.

Missy looked around the front room of Becky Lee's cottage. Still charming. Still inviting.

Nothing much had changed. Nostalgia swept over her and memories flooded back of all the times she'd hung out with her older cousin. She'd always been a bit jealous that Becky Lee had her own home and seemed so happy with her life. Of course Becky Lee had been one of those live in the moment, happy people since she was a young child. Missy envied that.

"Where do you want these?"

"The guest bedroom is down that hall on the left." Missy pointed.

Dylan disappeared down the hall and came back in a minute. "All set."

"Thanks for the help."

"You're more than welcome."

"So what are you up to these days?" Missy set down the guitar and turned to Dylan. "Still going out with Valerie?"

Dylan laughed. "Not exactly. We dated for a while after we all graduated, but she decided to head out for Chicago. Wanted the city life. She said there weren't enough opportunities in a small town. I guess she was a bit like you."

"Hey, it wasn't that I didn't like small-town life, I just wanted to try my hand at singing and songwriting. There is nothing wrong with Comfort Crossing. I miss the town."

"Point taken, sorry. Anyway, it looks like our foursome of you and Shawn, and me and Valerie is all busted up now. I kind of thought you'd end up with Shawn, Valerie and I would end up together and we'd stay a foursome."

"But Shawn married Belinda, I heard."

"He did. They are sickeningly sweet happy together and crazy about their kid, Billy." Dylan touched her arm. "Hey, you okay with that?"

"Oh, sure. Glad he's happy." Missy wasn't sure she was glad he was happy, but no need to show how petty she could be. Maybe she'd secretly hoped he was regretting his decision not to move to Nashville with her. Even pining away for her. But no, he was happily married, with a successful career, and an adorable kid to boot.

"I guess some couples are just not meant to be. Like you and Shawn, and me and Valerie."

"Guess not. We were so young then, too." Missy pasted on a don't-care-what-Shawn-did smile. "So, what do you do these days?"

"I work construction with Steve Bergeron, don't know if you remember him. Also help out Shawn a bit with the Christmas tree lot. I have an on again, off again gig at Frankie's."

"You're still singing?"

"Nothing as fancy as you, but yep, still singing

occasionally. I'm singing there tonight. Why don't you stop by?"

Frankie's. That's where she'd gotten her first taste of performing. Well, besides singing in the choir at church and some high school productions.

"Remember when we did that duet at the Variety Show in high school?" Dylan grinned. "We were great."

"Except the skit Shawn and the football players did singing that silly song took first place."

"And not a one of them could carry a tune. They had a campy, hilarious skit though."

Missy could remember wanting to be awarded first place in the Variety Show so badly back then. But it hadn't been meant to be. A lot of her hopes and dreams didn't seem to be meant to be.

"So you'll drop by tonight?" Dylan looked at her.

"Well, I'll check and see if my mom has anything planned. Though I'm sure she's baking all night for the tree lighting ceremony. A matter of fact, I should head over there now and help her out. I'll try to stop by tonight."

"That would be great. Hope to see you then."

❄

Dylan looked out over the crowd at Frankie's. He'd already finished one set and was taking a short break. He'd hoped Missy would show up. He knew he was just small time compared to her singing career, but he'd still hoped she'd drop by. He'd learned a lot since she'd left town. How to please a crowd, get them singing along, or quieted down when he sang a ballad. Maybe he even wanted to show off a bit for Missy.

She had looked good today. Still the quick smile even if a hint of sadness haunted the corners of it now. Her impossible curly brown hair she'd always said she'd trade in a flash for her cousin Becky Lee's long blonde hair. But he thought Missy's hair suited her personality, even if it had always annoyed her that it didn't ever cooperate how she'd planned. And Missy planned everything in her life. She'd planned to be a country singer since they'd been young kids and here she was, living the life in Nashville.

He sat at a table, nursing a beer, wondering what it would be like to be singing in Nashville. But then, he'd no desire to leave town. He was quite content with his life here in Comfort Crossing and his occasional gig at Frankie's.

"Hey, there." Shawn and Belinda walked up to him. "We got Belinda's mom to watch Billy tonight. Thought we'd have a night on the town. Went to Magnolia Cafe for dinner, then decided to catch you here." Shawn held out a chair for Belinda to sit in.

"Just taking a quick break."

"I'll be right back. Belinda, you want a beer?" Shawn rested his hand on her shoulder.

"Yes. A light one."

"As ever." Shawn leaned over and kissed the top of Belinda's head and she smiled.

Belinda shrugged off her jacket. "So, I hear Missy is back in town for Christmas."

"She is. I ran into her today. I invited her to come here tonight, but she wasn't sure if her mother had plans for them, or what."

"Oh, well, it will be good to see her if she does come." Belinda smiled.

Dylan detected no trace of jealousy or insecurity in Belinda's eyes. Just a woman confident in the love of her husband. It must be nice to have someone so in love with you and so secure in that love.

Dylan felt someone standing behind him and turned. "Missy, you did decide to come."

"I did." She smiled at him and turned to Belinda. "Good to see you, Belinda."

"It's been a long time." Belinda reached out her hand and Missy shook it.

Dylan jumped up and pulled out a chair for Missy. She slid into her seat, right as Shawn returned.

"Missy." Shawn froze for the briefest moment. "I heard you were in town. Good to see you." He put Belinda's beer down in front of her.

"I came by to catch Dylan's set."

"So did we." Shawn sat down beside his wife.

The four of them sat in silence for a moment.

"Can I get you—"

"Do you want—"

Dylan and Shawn spoke at the same time then laughed. Dylan stood up. "Let me get you a drink, Missy."

"Thanks. A beer is fine."

Dylan nodded and headed to the bar.

"So. You two got married." Missy shifted in her chair.

"We did. Five years ago in February." Belinda took a sip of her beer. "We have a son, Billy."

"He's a handful," Shawn added. "Cute, but a handful."

"That's nice."

"You've got that look that everyone gives me." Shawn leaned back and rested his arm across Belinda's shoulders. "The I-never-pictured-you-as-a-dad look."

"No. I… I didn't think that."

Belinda laughed. "Sure you did. Everyone does. But Shawn is a great dad."

"That's because we have such a great kid." Shawn pulled out his phone. "Want to see a picture?"

Missy didn't want him to know she'd been watching him with his son today out on Main Street and already knew how adorable he was, so she nodded.

Shawn scrolled through the photos and showed them to her, one by one.

"He's a cute kid," Missy said.

Belinda waved at someone across the room. "Hey, there's Jill. I'm going to pop over there and say hi." She got up and walked away from the table.

"So. You're back in town for the holidays." Shawn fiddled with a coaster on the table.

"Yes." Which was kind of true. No reason people had to know yet that she was planning on staying longer than that.

"Things going okay for you in Nashville?"

"Nashville is great." That wasn't a lie. Nashville *was* great. Just not for her. There was no way she was admitting to Shawn she'd come home in defeat. Not after seeing how he'd figured out his life like some kind of picture-perfect photograph of the ideal family.

"Good, I'm glad things have worked out for you, too." Shawn smiled and looked relieved. "So, we're all good here? Nothing awkward? We can still be friends?"

"Of course we can." What did he want her to say? But to be honest, she'd seen the way Shawn looked at Belinda, and he'd never looked at her in the same way. It was obvious the two of them were nuts about each other and their son.

Dylan walked up to the table and put her beer on the table. "I've got to go do another set. I'll catch you afterward?"

Missy nodded.

Belinda came back and perched on the chair next to Shawn, leaned over, and whispered something to him. Shawn smiled at her and squeezed her hand.

They did kind of look like the perfect couple.

Missy turned her attention to the stage in the

corner. Dylan sang a couple country songs. She sat and watched him and the people in Frankie's. Someone called out a request, and Dylan sang it. He stood up after the song and tapped the microphone.

"We have a special guest with us tonight at Frankie's. How about we give our own country singer, Missy Sherwood, a round of applause and see if she'll come up here and sing for us."

Missy was pretty sure she was about to kill Dylan. She looked around for a way to exit quickly.

"Go on, Missy. Go join Dylan." Shawn nodded towards the stage.

Missy sighed and stood up. She put on her best performance smile and crossed over to the stage. Dylan handed her his guitar and she perched on the stool by the microphone. "How about you join me, Dylan? We can sing the duet we did back in high school days."

The crowd clapped enthusiastically. Dylan grabbed another stool and sat next to her. She started out strumming the intro and started in on her part of the song. Dylan joined in on the chorus. For a while she lost herself in the moment. A crowd out front. Singing the lead instead of some vague backup singer. Their voices wound together and finished up with the ending of the song.

The crowd clapped and she heard Shawn's whistle from across the room.

"Thank you. Thank you. Now I think we'll persuade Missy to sing us one of her songs she's written. What do you say, Missy?"

She'd say she wanted to smack Dylan about right now, but another part of her was so darn glad to be able to perform one of her songs. She nodded and started a slow melody on the guitar. The words of the song drifted around her, lyrics about making choices in life and the roads a person takes. The crowd grew silent as she sang the song. Even the people playing pool across the room stood quietly and listened. Listened to the words she'd written for the haunting melody she'd created. She finished the song and Frankie's patrons burst into applause.

The sound wrapped around her like a familiar, comfortable quilt. She'd missed the applause. The applause for her, not some other singer. She smiled at the crowd and let the feeling wash over her. The day had certainly turned out better than she expected. Tonight was just... wonderful.

CHAPTER 3

"Wow, you sure haven't lost your voice." Shawn leaned across the table as Missy sat back down.

"That song was beautiful. You wrote it? You have such a talent. Both music and words." Belinda smiled at her.

"Thank you." Missy didn't know what to say. She was still basking in the applause.

Dylan sang a few more songs and ended his set. He came over and sat beside her. "That was fun, wasn't it? Singing together again? And your song was great."

"Thank you. It was fun to sing with you again." She eyed Dylan over her beer glass. "But you shouldn't have waylaid me like that."

"I was afraid if I asked you beforehand, you'd

say no. But I knew you wouldn't walk away once they started clapping for you to come up."

"You're a sly one, Dylan Rivers."

He winked at her. "Well, it worked."

Shawn and Belinda stood up. "We better head home. We told Belinda's mother we wouldn't be late. Gotta go gather up our little guy. I've got an early day at the tree lot tomorrow." Shawn paused and smiled. "It was good to see you again, Missy."

"Same here." Missy realized it had been good to see Shawn. Shawn and Belinda. Somehow seeing how happy they were together had brought a kind of closure to that portion of her life. The portion that had always wondered "what if."

"They are a great couple, aren't they?" Dylan nodded towards Shawn and Belinda as they wound their way across Frankie's towards the door.

"They are. They seem just perfect for each other."

Frankie herself came up to their table with two beers in her hand. "Here you go, you two. The set was great. Dylan knows he's welcome here anytime, but Missy, you're welcome to sing here anytime, too." She set the beers on the table. "On the house. Enjoy. And if you've got any more time while you're in town, you come by here and do a set for us, okay?"

"Thanks, Frankie." Missy smiled at the woman. Frankie had to be fifty years old. Short. Slender. Always had on slim jeans, cowboy boots, and a Frankie's t-shirt. Not much had changed here over the years either.

Dylan raised his beer glass to hers. "To a good set."

They clinked beer mugs and then sipped their drinks. Missy enjoyed the easy camaraderie she and Dylan shared. It was like they'd slipped right back into their friendship of years ago. She was glad to have a friend here in town.

"I guess I should be heading back to Becky Lee's. It's getting late."

"Did you drive or walk over?"

"I walked. Love being able to walk to so many places here. Besides, I feel safe walking around Comfort Crossing after dark."

"Well, how about I walk you back to Becky Lee's anyway?"

"Sure." Missy stood up and put on her jacket. She followed Dylan to the door, pausing a few times while he spoke to people at tables. Each time the people said they'd enjoyed her song, too. It was nice. Very nice.

❄

It was a nice night for a walk. Dylan assured himself that was all this was. But, if he were honest with himself, he really enjoyed Missy's company. He'd forgotten how easy she was to talk to.

They strolled down Main Street, popping in and out of the light from the street lamps lining the street. White Christmas lights were strung across the street at intervals. Red bows were tied on each and every lamp post. He really enjoyed this time of year. The town looked so festive and people were extra friendly.

"So are you going to go to the tree lighting ceremony tomorrow night?" Dylan finally broke the companionable silence.

"Wouldn't miss it. Besides, I'm sure mom will wrangle me into hauling over the bazillion dozens of cookies she made. You going?"

"Of course. Never miss it. I'm letting the kids out early from the play practice for it."

"You're heading up the kids' pageant this year?"

"I am as of this week. Miss Judy who usually does it got called out of town. Had to go take care of her mother. She begged me to take over so the show could go on. I will say, I'm not the best kid wrangler out there." Dylan turned to Missy. "Hey, you want to help me out? We meet at four at the town hall. I sure could use the help."

"Oh, I don't know. I'm not that great with kids, myself." Missy's brown eyes looked doubtful.

"Please don't make me beg..."

Missy laughed. "Okay, I'll be there at four and see if I can help any. I remember doing the pageant when we were kids. They still doing the play about when a stranger came to Comfort Crossing for Christmas?"

"We are. With a few changes here and there, but basically the same story." Dylan paused under a street lamp. "A stranger comes to town and when people tell him what they want for Christmas, their wishes come true. You know, my grandmother swore it's based on a true story. Happened years ago right here in Comfort Crossing."

"Well, any way you look at it, it's a charming part of our town's history whether it's based in fact or not."

"Yep, it is." Dylan started walking again. "And I'll sure be glad to have your help."

❄

Missy said goodnight to Dylan and slipped into Becky Lee's home.

"I'm back here." Becky Lee's voice drifted through the house.

Missy hung her jacket on a coat tree by the door and headed back to the kitchen. Becky Lee sat at the table with a cup of tea and her feet propped up on a kitchen chair.

"Long day?"

"It was. Grab yourself a teacup from the cabinet and join me."

Missy fixed a cup of tea and sat down at the table.

"I got your note that said you went to Frankie's. Did you have a good time?"

"I did. Dylan was playing there. Ran into Shawn and Belinda, too."

"How did that go?" Becky Lee took a sip of her tea.

"It actually was… okay. They seem really happy together."

"They do."

"I thought it would be awkward, but it was okay. They're perfect for each other. And I realized that Shawn and I, well, we weren't perfect. He never looked at me the way he looks at Belinda. I mean, I guess we were in love, in a young kid kind of way, but what he has with Belinda just seems like so much more."

"Well, I'm glad it wasn't awkward for you. I'm sure you'll run into him a lot during the holidays. Hard to avoid running into people in Comfort Crossing."

"In my mind I thought he'd be sitting back here in town, pining away for me, regretting his decision to not come with me to Nashville. Instead he was here growing his business, settling down, and has one heck of an adorable kid. But I'm happy for him."

"Good for you. To be honest, I could never see you two as long-term together. There wasn't ever that big spark between you."

"Really?" Missy considered what Becky Lee had said. Maybe she was right. Maybe they'd fallen into an easy, familiar high school boyfriend-girlfriend routine.

"So, you have anyone you're serious about back in Nashville?"

"Nope. I've dated off and on. Mostly off. But no one seriously. How about you?"

"No one serious." Becky Lee set her teacup down and stood up, stretching. "I'm headed to bed. Have a full day tomorrow. You going to the tree lighting?"

"I am. Right after I help Dylan with the pageant practice."

Becky Lee grinned. "So, you got roped into that already? Good for you. I'm sure he could use your help. I helped out Miss Judy one year and I swear, she can keep those kids in line with just a look while still letting them be kids and have a blast. Me? Not so much."

"Now, don't go scaring me off. I guess we'll see how well I do with it tomorrow."

"I guess we will." Becky Lee laughed and headed down the hallway. "See you in the morning. Good to have you here."

CHAPTER 4

Missy was surprised, or more likely stunned, at how much she enjoyed the pageant practice with the kids. She had the kids sing their songs, reciting the few lines scattered through the play. Timmy Hardy, a cute little kid of about eight or nine was playing the part of the stranger.

"Miss Sherwood, I'm gonna forget my lines. I just know it." Timmy sat on the edge of the stage during a quick snack break they were taking. "My brother Jeremy says so."

"Well, not to disagree with your brother, but I think you'll do fine. You're doing great with your lines at practice today."

"I get kind of scared about messing up."

"You know, I get kind of scared too when I go up on stage with my music, but once I get going the scared goes away."

"So you'll help me get going at the pageant?"

"I sure will. I'll be right there."

"Wait 'til I tell Jeremy you're gonna help me. I'll be the best stranger guy ever." Timmy jumped up. "Hey, I'm going to go have some of your momma's cookies you brought."

Missy wasn't sure all the parents would appreciate her feeding cookies to their kids when they were sure to fill up on them again tonight at the tree lighting ceremony, but she'd wanted to win them over. The cookies sure seemed to be helping.

Dylan walked over to where she sat on the edge of the stage. "You are absolutely amazing with these kids. You've gotten more accomplished in the last hour than I did all week. You're great with them."

"I'm having a blast." Missy smiled. "Who knew?"

"So did you soothe Timmy's nerves? He doesn't really have many lines, but he's worried about them. He takes his part so seriously."

"I think so. I told him I'd be there for him."

"Like I said. You're a miracle worker."

Missy stood up. "Well, let's get a bit more practice finished before we declare me that, how about it?"

"I'll round up the kids if I can tear them away from your mom's cookies."

Missy watched as Dylan headed over to the table of cookies, swiped one for himself and led the kids back to the stage, joking and laughing with them as he got them back into their places.

They wound up the practice with the traditional singing of Silent Night, which was how the pageant had ended for years, with all the audience joining in.

"Okay, kids. I'll see you all tomorrow. You did great. Tomorrow we'll do a dress rehearsal." Missy watched as the kids gathered their jackets and jostled each other, laughing and calling to each other.

"That went well." Dylan stooped to pick up a prop.

"It did. I hope the dress rehearsal goes as well tomorrow."

"A handful of moms have promised to come help wrestle them into the costumes."

"Oh, good. I'm sure we'll need the help."

Missy picked up a star that had fallen from the background and stuck it back into place. "I'd better hurry home. I promised Mom I'd help her haul the cookies to the park and set up the snack table."

"Guess I'll see you there tonight, then."

"Yes, I'll see you tonight."

Missy found her mother in the kitchen, boxing up the last of the cookies. "Mom, it looks like you made enough to feed the town for weeks."

"I'm not the only one bringing cookies tonight and some of these are for the Christmas party at the nursing home. Remember our old neighbor, Mrs. Greene? She's lived at the nursing home the last few years and I've been going to the party each year. You'll go with me this year, won't you? I'm sure she'd love to see you. I help out a bit with the music, too."

"Of course I'll go. I'd love to see her, too."

"Living at home alone just got a bit too much for her. She seems happy at the nursing home. She's made friends, of course. Plays bridge twice a week with a group there. I try to get by to see her as often as possible."

Missy watched as her mother boxed up the last of the cookies, humming a Christmas carol under her breath as she bustled around the kitchen. Her mother was one of the most giving, kindest women she knew. Always giving of her time. Or her baking. Her mother loved to bake for anyone and everyone.

It felt so right to be in the kitchen again with her mom, listening to her humming a song and standing there among the mountains of cookies in her predictable but ridiculous Christmas sweater.

"Here, Mom, let me load up."

They wrestled the boxes of cookies into the car and over to the cookie table at the park. People were beginning to gather. Christmas lights lit up the gazebo in the center of the park. Kids dashed this way and that. A few rushed by her with calls of "Hi, Miss Sherwood."

"The kids seem taken with you." Her mother nodded towards a set of twins who raced by and said hi.

"They were great. I really had a good time working with them on the pageant today."

"I'm glad you're here to help out." Her mother wrapped one arm around her and hugged her. "And I'm really glad you're home for

Christmas. It hasn't seemed like a real Christmas without you."

"I'm glad I'm home, too, Mom." She wondered what her mom would say when she learned the move was permanent. She just had to find the right time to tell her. Explain how she hadn't been able to make it in Nashville. Oh, and she needed to find a job.

Dylan scanned the park, looking for Missy. The park was crowded with townsfolk laughing, sipping hot chocolate, and munching on cookies. He saw the mayor head to the gazebo for his annual Christmas speech.

"Hey, you." Missy sidled up beside him in the crowd.

"There you are." Dylan smiled at her. "I couldn't find you in the mass of people. Comfort Crossing sure does like their tree lighting."

"I admit I'm kind of excited. Haven't been to the tree lighting in years. It was always one of my favorite nights growing up."

"Glad you made it back this year." He *was* pleased she'd come home this year. She was helping him with the pageant, right? That's why he was so happy she was back in town. That was all it was.

The mayor climbed up on the gazebo and welcomed the crowd. He signaled the high school band beside the gazebo and they started playing Silent Night. All the people joined in the singing.

Dylan glanced down at Missy, standing by his side. Her eyes were wide with joy as she sang along. He watched while she slowly looked around the crowd as she sang and gave a little wave when she spied her mother. Her mom waved back.

As the music ended, he saw her clasp her hands and look towards the large evergreen beside the gazebo. After a moment of silence where it seemed like everyone in the crowd was holding their breath, the tree came alive with lights and a brightly lit star on top. Missy stood silent, her eyes gleaming. He saw her swipe away a lone tear.

"You okay?"

"I am. I'd just forgotten how wonderful the tree lighting is. How much I've missed it."

He gave her a quick hug. "It is definitely one of the perks of living in Comfort Crossing."

The band started playing Deck the Halls, and the people started milling around again, talking to neighbors and friends. Dylan and Missy wandered over to the snack table and Missy's mom pressed cups of hot chocolate into their hands.

"Here. Missy always did love the hot chocolate part of the tree lighting ceremony."

"I love every part of it." Missy eyes shone with excitement.

"I'm glad you're having a good time." Her mother smiled at Missy. "Dwayne is going to help me load up after the crowd thins out. So you just enjoy yourself."

"Thanks, Mom. I will."

"And why don't you come over for coffee in the morning. We'll have a chance to catch up before everyone arrives for the holiday and things get crazy."

"I will. I'd like that." Missy pressed a kiss on her mother's cheek.

They strolled through the park, saying hi to friends and sipping on their chocolate. When they finished their drinks and tossed the cups into the trash can, he noticed Missy shiver. "You cold?"

"Just a bit."

He took her two hands between his and rubbed them quickly.

"Your hands are so warm." Missy kept her hands in his while he warmed them, then took her hands and pushed them into the pockets of her jacket. "Much better."

"I'll walk you home now and you can get all warmed up."

"Aren't you tired of walking me home yet?"

He grinned. "Not yet. But I'll let you know if it wears me out." He tucked a hand on her elbow and led her out of the park and onto the brightly lit Main Street.

Missy liked hanging out with Dylan. He was funny, charming, and it was just so easy to be with him. She was glad he'd offered to walk her back to Becky Lee's because she wasn't ready for the night to end yet. The tree lighting had been magical. The Christmas play practice had gone great. All in all, it had been one of the better days she'd had in a long, long time.

"You want to come in for a bit?" Missy stood paused in the doorway to her cousin's house. The front porch was awash with a twinkling glow from the Christmas lights her cousin had strung around her windows.

"I could for a bit." Dylan followed her into the house.

Missy stopped and plugged in the lights on the Christmas tree and the front room flooded with a cheerful glow. "I just love the Christmas lights."

"Do you have a big tree back in Nashville?"

"Not exactly. Honestly, not even close. It's actually a tree that the Christmas tree lot people had thrown out because most of the branches were broken."

Dylan's brow creased. "Really? I figured you had this fancy apartment there with store-bought decorations and… I don't know."

"No, my life isn't like that. I share—*did share*—an apartment with two friends. A walkup in a debatably decent neighborhood." Missy steeled herself for the inevitable look of disappointment that was coming. "I've been more like a receptionist, waitress, store clerk than a singer. I haven't had a singing gig in months."

Dylan stood there quietly, but to his credit, he wasn't giving her any pitying looks.

"The last job I had? The company went out of business. I'd given myself until the end of this year to either make it or realize I didn't have what it takes and move on with my life. Find something else to do other than being a singer or songwriter. I figured losing this last job was a sign. I hardly have any savings. I didn't know where else to go, so I headed home."

"I don't know what to say. I'm sorry. I'm sure it's tough. I think you've said you wanted to be a country singer since... well, ever since I've known you."

"I guess I just don't have what it takes. Or never got my lucky break. Or something..." Disappointment rushed through her. Saying it all out loud made it seem so real. Terribly real. "I thought I had my life all planned out, you're right. But it just hasn't worked out how I intended. I guess the universe is laughing at me about now."

"Maybe the universe has other plans for your life. Something you haven't thought of."

"I guess so because life sure isn't working out the way I thought it would." Missy headed toward the kitchen. "Come on. Let's raid the fridge and see if Becky Lee has some beer for us."

Time to change the subject and move on. Now Dylan knew she'd failed. Soon everyone in town would know.

She felt Dylan's hand on her arm and turned to look at him.

"You know, you're not a failure just because things didn't work out like you intended. Sometimes life has other plans for us, ones we haven't thought of before. I really believe we end up where we're supposed to be."

"Maybe." But Missy wasn't so sure of that. Because if she wasn't going to be a country singer… not on any level, not even a backup singer, then what was she going to do with her life? Her music had been her whole focus for as long as she could remember.

CHAPTER 5

"I'm so sorry, honey." Missy's mom sat across the kitchen table from her. She set her cup down and reached for Missy's hand. "I know you always dreamed of being a country singer."

Missy felt a catch in her throat. She did not want to break into tears in front of her mother. "It just didn't work out for me. I tried. I tried so hard. Auditions, open mic nights, demos of my songs sent everywhere. I just couldn't make it happen."

"Well, I firmly believe that when one door closes, another one opens."

"I don't have any idea what I'm going to do now." Her heart thumped dully in her chest

"We'll sort it all out. You know you're welcome to stay here for as long as you need to."

How could she do that without feeling like an

even bigger failure? A grown woman moving back in with her mother? "Thanks, Mom. We'll see."

"I still feel bad that we'll have the house all filled up with Dwayne's family for the holidays. You know we could still fit you in the den on the pull-out sofa. I love his family, they've all been so accepting of me, but I still feel terrible that the rooms will be filled."

"I'm good at Becky Lee's. I think she even likes the company for the holidays." Which reminded Missy that she hadn't told Becky Lee the move back to Comfort Crossing was permanent. Once again with the whole I-couldn't-make-it conversation. She could feel her pulse thudding in her temple and she reached up one hand to massage it.

"Don't you worry, dear. We'll figure everything out after Christmas. I hope you can just relax and enjoy the holidays for now."

"I'll try." Missy set down her coffee cup and stood up. "I've got to run now. I want to look through the costumes for the play and work on some of the set decorations." What she really needed was some time alone. Time to think.

"I'll see you later, then?"

"I'll check in later today." Missy walked out of her mother's house. The house that didn't feel like home to her, not that Dwayne wasn't anything but welcoming to her. She just didn't know where she fit in these days.

Missy walked down the street and crossed through the town park. It had been transformed from a magical tree lighting place to a town park in the bright light of day. She sat on a bench and watched a few young kids swing on the swings and slide down the slides, their mothers sitting together on a nearby bench, watching over them.

"Mind if I join you?" An older man with a red jacket and cabled scarf stood in the glare of the sunshine.

"Um, of course." There were maybe a half dozen other benches scattered throughout the park. Why did this guy want to sit with her?

"You looked kind of sad. I don't mean to intrude."

Where were her manners? Everyone was nice to everyone in Comfort Crossing. "No, please, sit down."

"Don't mind if I do." The man sat on the bench and stretched out his legs. "I'm Mr. Nick."

"Nice to meet you, Mr. Nick. I'm Missy."

He watched the kids playing on the playground and smiled. "Those mothers are probably trying to wear off some of the pre-

Christmas energy with those young tykes. They've probably already made up their Christmas lists." The man chuckled. "And changed their minds quite a few times."

"I remember when I was a little girl I would carefully plan out what to ask Santa for each year."

"A planner, huh? Well, what are you asking Santa for this year?"

Missy looked at the man sitting beside her. "Well, every year for as long as I can remember I've wished to become a country singer." She felt a warm blush creep over her face.

"Well, I bet you get your Christmas wish this year."

"I don't think so. I've kind of given up on it."

"Maybe it's time to make a new list. Maybe it's not truly your wish anymore, and it's time to wish for something else."

"That's the problem. I don't know what I want anymore." Missy stared down at her hands.

"Ah, maybe you'll get something for Christmas you didn't even know you needed and wanted. Christmas wishes are like that sometimes."

Missy looked across the park at the kids and their mothers. Living their lives. Happy. How had she managed to make herself so miserable in Nashville? "Maybe it *is* time for a new list."

"Well, I better be going." Mr. Nick stood up and wrapped the scarf around his neck, the ends of it hanging jauntily across his ample belly. "Nice talking with you."

"Nice talking with you, too."

Missy watched as the man strolled down the pathway, stopped to talk for a moment with the moms on the bench, and headed out of the park.

Dylan helped Missy clean up after the Christmas play practice. Things were coming together nicely. The kids had loved wearing their costumes today.

"That old coat Timmy is wearing as the stranger is huge on him." Missy stood on the stage, holding up the coat.

"But did you see how much he loved wearing it?"

Missy laughed. "I did. Even when his brother Jeremy told him he looked like a dork."

"Didn't hurt that little Anna piped up and said he looked handsome in it."

"It did kind of make him have a swagger to his walk after that, didn't it?" Missy hung up the coat on the rack of costumes at the side of the stage. "I was so proud of all of them today. I think the play is really coming together."

"Thanks to your help. Seriously, I just had constant chaos when I tried to hold the rehearsals. You have a magical way with them."

"Well, I'm having a really good time." Missy looked around the stage. "I think that's everything."

"Do you want to go to Magnolia Cafe with me and catch some dinner?" Dylan realized he was holding his breath just a bit, waiting for her answer.

"Sure. Mom and Dwayne have some kind of business party they are going to. They invited me, but I turned down the offer. Pretty sure Mom thinks she has to keep an eye on me all the time to see if I fall apart." Missy paused and looked directly at him. "I told her about Nashville. How I couldn't cut it there and I was moving back here."

"And I bet she was great about it. Supportive. I'm sure she's excited to have you back here in town."

"She was great, of course. She's always so supportive of anything I do. She reminded me that when one door closes, another opens." Missy paused and looked across the stage. "I just wish I knew where to look for that opening door."

"You'll figure it out."

"Hope it's sooner than later." Missy grabbed her jacket. "Let's go, I'm starving. I'm getting a burger and topping dinner off with a piece of pecan pie."

"I think I'll have the same."

They walked to Magnolia Cafe and pushed through the doors into the cheerfully lit restaurant. Becky Lee waved and motioned for them to grab a table. They sat at a table by the window.

Becky Lee dropped off two glasses of water. "Menus?"

"Nope. We're good." Dylan leaned back in his seat.

"Be right back for your order." Becky Lee handled two tables then returned to them. "Guess y'all know what you want, huh?"

"Two burgers, two fries. Pecan pie for dessert." Dylan placed their order. "What do you want to drink?"

"I'll have sweet tea."

"Same for me."

Becky Lee hurried away, grabbing a handful of dirty dishes from a table, and pausing to say something to her friends Jenny and Bella sitting at a table in the corner.

"Becky Lee can handle about ninety-nine things at once." Missy nodded towards her cousin.

"I'll say." Dylan watched at how effortlessly Becky Lee dealt with all her customers.

"Plus she's taken in her wayward cousin now, too." Missy glanced out the window, but not before he saw the pain chasing the corners of her eyes.

She must be so disappointed. A planner never did well when their plans were all blown to heck. "I am sorry about Nashville." He reached over and touched her hand.

Missy straightened her shoulders and turned back to look at him. "I am, too. But it's time to move on."

He left his hand resting on hers when she turned and looked out the window. He squeezed her hand once in a show of silent support.

"May I walk you home?" Dylan flashed a lazy grin at her.

"Yet again?" She smiled back at him.

"Wouldn't want you to get lost."

"In a town I grew up in and could probably find my way around it blindfolded?"

"Yes, that town." He winked at her.

"Well, I hate getting lost, so I'll accept your offer." Missy tugged on her jacket and they left the Magnolia Cafe.

The night had turned cool and a light breeze had picked up. The strings of Christmas lights strung across the street swayed in the wind. Missy fastened her jacket and made a mental note to borrow some warmer clothes from Becky Lee. She was going to have to go back to Nashville soon and get the rest of her things, including some warmer sweaters.

Dylan draped his arm around her shoulder as they walked. "I think I'm going to go out and buy you some warmer clothes."

"I was just thinking of raiding Becky Lee's closet. I'll have to head back to Nashville and get the rest of my things. Guess I'll do that after the holidays."

"So, you really are planning on staying here?"

"I guess so. I'll need to find a job, and not sure what I'll do. Not much call for an unemployed singer-songwriter here in town."

"You can at least get some gigs at Frankie's.

Doesn't pay much, but it's fun to get in front of a crowd."

"I'll definitely talk to her about that, but I need something steady to pay the bills."

"I'm sure you'll find something."

Missy wasn't so sure. Her experience in the last few years had been multiple receptionist positions, from a hair styling salon to a small travel company. Oh, and then various waitressing jobs at a busy diner, and then onto a wannabe country bar that didn't even fill all their seats on the weekends. Missy let a deep sigh slip out before she could stop it.

"What would you like to do? You have to have some other interests besides singing."

"I never really thought of what else I could do with my life. I know I seem a bit old to be thinking about what I want to do when I grow up."

"Not at all. People readjust their thinking all through their lives. Plans change. Life sometimes throws you an unexpected curve."

"If I can find something to tide me over for a bit, I'll try to figure out a long-term solution after that…"

"And there you have it. A plan." Dylan flashed her a self-satisfied smile like he'd solved all her problems.

Maybe it solved some short-term problem, but it didn't help with the what-to-do-with-her-life problem. She was used to having a carefully laid out life map. She held back another sigh, unwilling to have a pity party.

She was a planner, she'd figure it all out again.

Dylan stood with Missy on Becky Lee's front porch and for the life of him, couldn't figure out why he wanted to kiss the woman standing next to him. They'd been friends forever. Oh, he might have had a high-school crush on Missy that was quickly squashed when she started dating his best friend, Shawn. *Might have*. But this desire to pull her into his arms was nuts. She'd only been back a handful of days.

He carefully took a step back, putting some distance between them.

"Well, I better go in. Going over to Mom's in the morning to help wrap up some presents for the nursing home residents. Mom got her knitting friends to knit and crochet up some lap blankets and a handful of other fun presents for residents who don't get many visitors. Evidently she's been doing this for a few years, ever since our old neighbor, Mrs. Greene, moved there. She doesn't have any family left and Mom took to visiting her and now has a bunch of residents she's made friends with."

"Your mother is one of the kindest people I've ever met."

"You're right there. She always has time for everyone, always helping. I hope I have one-tenth of her energy when I get to her age." Missy laughed. "Heck, I'd take that energy now."

"You seem to be following in her footsteps."

Missy looked surprised. "What do you mean?"

"Helping out with the Christmas play. Setting up for the tree lighting ceremony. Helping your mom wrap presents for the nursing home..."

"I..." Missy's brow crinkled. "I guess so. But I'm enjoying helping. I can't believe how much fun the pageant rehearsals are. Watching the kids' eyes light up as they conquer more of their lines. And watching them in their costumes, they had such a good time at the dress rehearsal."

"Timmy is convinced you're going to be the magic that helps him remember his lines. He's so proud that he gets to play the stranger this year."

"He's going to do great. Just needs a bit of encouragement."

"Well, I think you're a big part of that. He's

really taken to you."

"He's a great kid. They all are."

"Now that you've sorted it all out and gotten the play organized. I was a disaster when I was put in charge. Why they thought that just because I can sing I could run the play, I'll never know. Okay, the play *does* have songs in it, but that's about the extent of what I could sort out for them."

The Christmas lights on the front window bathed them both in twinkling, magic light.

No, they didn't.

Dylan took another step back and shoved his hands in his pockets. "I better let you go in then. Sounds like you have a busy day."

Missy cracked open the door, then turned back to him. "See you at rehearsal?"

"Yep, see you then."

Missy walked into the house and he was left standing alone with his thoughts. With his regrets. He should have kissed her when he had the chance. Then he shook his head. Missy was going to stay in town, he had all the time in the world to take things slowly with her and see what happened between them.

He walked down the sidewalk to the street, whistling a Christmas carol.

CHAPTER 6

"Mom, you have a mountain of presents here." Missy looked at the stack of gifts they'd wrapped, and the pile of things still left to be wrapped and decorated with the festive ribbon her mother insisted be tied on each and every gift.

"There are so many residents at the nursing home who have no one visiting them for the holidays. Either their families are out of town, or they are the last one left in their family. I like to make sure everyone gets a gift or two."

Her mother had a whole system set up with the wrapping paper so she would know which gifts were for males, which were for females, and which were for either. Then she had a stack of presents she'd specifically picked out for some of the residents and carefully tagged with their names.

"You'll help me at the Christmas party, won't you?" Her mother paused, a strip of tape hanging from one finger, her other hand firmly holding the paper closed at the end of a box.

"Sure, I will. I think it'll be great."

Missy looked over at the large box of wrapping paper her mother had next to the table. "Did you get all that on sale after Christmas last year?"

"Of course. I never pay full price for wrapping paper." Her mother looked shocked at the very idea.

Missy grinned. "No, I suppose you don't."

"A penny saved is a penny earned." Her mother deftly sealed up another gift.

Two things she could count on from her mother. Bargain shopping and an adage for every situation.

Missy stood up and stretched, surprised to see how many hours they'd been working at wrapping the presents.

"I'm going to have to wrap things up here…" Missy paused and smiled at her unintended pun. "I need to get over to rehearsal. Going to hem up the Mrs. Claus skirt. Evidently this year's Mrs. Claus is much shorter than last years'. Don't want her tripping on stage."

"Well, I appreciate the help, dear. You have fun."

Missy left her mother's house and got to the town hall in time to hem up the skirt before the kids started drifting in for practice.

Missy and Dylan headed over to Frankie's after the play practice. It was getting to be a nice routine Missy enjoyed, spending time with Dylan.

They ordered up burgers and fries and sat at a table enjoying the bustle around them and laughing about the kids and the play.

"I think even Timmy is going to get his lines memorized." Dylan grinned.

"I think so, too. He's trying so hard."

Frankie walked up to their table. "Hey, you two. Good to see you in again."

"Hi, Frankie." Missy set down her burger and wiped her hands on her napkin.

"I've got a favor to ask. Couple of them, actually."

"Shoot." Missy looked at Frankie.

"Well, I wondered if you two could do a set later tonight. The crowd loved you." Frankie looked at both of them.

"How about if just Missy does tonight? Let her do a solo act."

"Fine by me. Does that work for you, Missy?"

"You sure, Dylan?"

"I'd actually love to hear you sing. Why don't you take this one tonight?"

Frankie grinned. "Okay, one more favor. I need an act for New Year's Eve. Could you two cover that?"

Missy looked over at Dylan.

"Works for me." Dylan reached out and shook Frankie's hand. "New Year's Eve it is."

"Thanks. I'm sure we'll have a big crowd that night. Maybe we could set up some regular work for you two?"

"I'd like that." Missy felt a sense of relief. At least she'd be bringing in a little something until she could figure out a job and a way to earn more money.

"Great. Well, I don't want to interrupt your meal. I'll see you up on stage in a bit?"

"Yes." Missy looked down at her plate and lost her appetite. Nervous flutters drifted across her stomach.

Dylan looked at her and laughed. "Got a case of the nerves?"

"A bit. I mean when you called me up there the other night I didn't even have time to get anxious."

"You'll do great. You'll see." Dylan attacked his burger with gusto.

She sat and picked at her fries and tried to decide which songs she should sing. Dylan just sat across from her and grinned at her nervousness.

Dylan watched while Missy went up on stage and got ready to sing a set. Hadn't taken much encouragement from Frankie to coax her into it. Maybe Missy could be happy here in Comfort Crossing, singing some at Frankie's, finding a job.

Shawn slid into the seat across from him and handed him a beer. "So, Frankie talked her into singing again?"

"Sure did."

"You two have sure been seeing a lot of each other while she's been in town."

"Some."

"When is she leaving to go back to Nashville?" Shawn glanced up toward the stage.

"She's not."

"Not leaving?" Shawn set down his beer mug. "Really?"

"Really. She's staying in Comfort Crossing."

"I thought she wanted to be a big country singer star."

Dylan looked at his friend, not sure what to say because it wasn't his story to tell. It was Missy's.

Shawn cocked his head to the side and stared at him. "Okay, that was always her dream, so I have to guess she couldn't make it happen. That's too bad. So she's really moving back?"

"She is."

"You know, living here in this small town has never been her dream. I hope you're being careful. I know how you were after Valerie left to move to Chicago."

"This is different." Dylan stared down into his beer mug, wondering if it really was different this time. If the small town of Comfort Crossing really could hold Missy's interest. He'd been gutted when Valerie left. He hadn't been enough to make her want to stay. He'd barely dated in the years since then, now look at him. Falling for a woman whose dream was in Nashville. *Was.* She said that dream was over.

Shawn shook his head. "Whatever you say, buddy. Just be careful."

Dylan sat and listened to Missy's set, watching her eyes light up when the crowd clapped, watching the wide smile she wore after each song. Watching her come alive.

He turned and looked at Shawn. His friend just shrugged and sipped his drink.

"Will you go out on an actual date with me tomorrow?" Dylan stood, once again, on Becky Lee's front porch.

Missy's eyes widen. "A date, date?"

"Yep. The real kind. I pick you up. We go out. A date-date."

"Um… sure."

"Don't sound so enthusiastic." Dylan rolled his eyes and grinned at her.

"No, I mean…" Missy let out a little huff of air. "Yes. That would be fun."

Not exactly the eager acceptance he'd been hoping for, but he'd take what he could get.

"So I'll pick you up about six tomorrow night. Give you time to get home after rehearsal and do whatever it is women do to get ready for a date.

They have a nice restaurant in that plantation out of town. Did you know they turned the old plantation into a resort?"

"No, I hadn't heard. That sounds nice."

"Good, it's a date then." He winked at her. "A date-date."

CHAPTER 7

Missy stood in front of Becky Lee's closet as Becky Lee rummaged through it, pulling out outfits. "How about this one?" Becky held up a simple black knit dress. "I have this red jacket you can wear with it. Very Christmasy."

"I appreciate this. I didn't really bring enough clothes with me. I've got to get back to Nashville and get them."

"You take your time on sorting things out. You can stay here as long as you need to."

Missy looked over at her cousin. She'd been so supportive when Missy had told her she was moving back to Comfort Crossing and why. Becky Lee knew just about every single person in town, and with a steady stream of people coming and going through the Magnolia Cafe, she said she'd put out feelers to see if they could turn up a job for Missy.

"And I have a closet full you're welcome to borrow any time." Becky Lee looked at her watch. "I've gotta run, but y'all have fun tonight."

"We will." Missy held up the dress in front of her and looked in the mirror. "I mean, I hope we will. I don't know. Dylan. He asked me on a real date. I was so surprised."

Becky Lee laughed. "Of course he did. Didn't you know he had a crush on you in high school?"

Missy whirled around and stared at her cousin. "He did not."

"Ah, my clueless cousin. He did. But you started dating Shawn and that whole best friends guy code kicked in."

"But he dated Valerie."

"That was after you and Shawn were already a thing."

"I didn't know…"

"You were too besotted with Shawn, who was the wrong guy for you, by the way. Everyone could see that but you." Becky Lee picked up her purse and headed toward the bedroom door. "The guy has waited years to ask you out… at least let the poor guy show you a good time."

Missy slipped into the dress and a pair of

black heels she'd thankfully thrown in her suitcase. She curled her hair and carefully applied her makeup. She had a date. With Dylan. Dylan, the person Becky Lee swore had a crush on her. Missy shook her head. No, that can't be right. She would have known.

She couldn't have been that clueless, could she?

Dylan was pretty sure he'd made a fool of himself on the date. He'd spilled his glass of wine all over the table. Red wine. Their easy-going conversations of the last days had ended. Most of his answers to her questions had been simple yeses and nos when he could even get his words out.

Missy had kept looking at him, with those brown eyes, and he'd lost all his senses. He carefully set down his water glass, fairly certain Missy would never go out with him again, much less stay his friend, his pal.

"Dylan. You want to tell me what's going on?" Missy sat staring at him, pinning him with a tell-me-now look.

"What do you mean?" He fidgeted in his

chair, at the same time telling himself to sit still and quit acting like a dolt.

"Ever since I've been home, we've had so much fun together. I felt like I could talk to you about anything. But tonight? It's like carrying on a one-sided conversation."

"I know. I'm sorry."

"We shouldn't have called it a real date. It's ruined us." The corners of Missy's mouth hinted at a grin.

He let out a long, drawn-out breath. "You're right. That's my problem."

"Then, how about we call it a non-date date?" This time a grin spread all across her face.

"If that will stop me from acting like such a blockhead, I'm up for calling it a non-date date."

"A non-date it is."

And just like that, Missy broke the awkwardness, and they slipped back into their easy camaraderie. He told her all about the house he was working on with Steve Bergeron. They were putting the finishing touches on it, rushing to get it finished early, so the buyers could move in before Christmas. She told him about her life in Nashville and her roommates.

By the time dinner was over, he'd almost forgotten what a fool he'd made of himself.

Almost. He drove her back to Becky Lee's and walked her to the door.

"I had a really good time." Missy stood in the glow of the Christmas lights. "You know, after you stopped acting all nervous."

He laughed then, an easy-going, carefree laugh. Without giving it much thought—oh, who was he kidding, he'd thought about it the whole drive back from dinner—he leaned over, tilted her head up and kissed her. His heart jolted in his chest, catching him off guard.

She kissed him back, softly and tentatively. Then her arm wound around his neck and he deepened the kiss.

She finally pulled back and touched her lips. "I... wasn't expecting that."

"Because it was a non-date date now?" He was surprised he could even find his words.

"No, I wasn't expecting to... *feel*... that."

He sucked in a breath of the charged air between them. "You felt it, too?"

She looked straight into his eyes. "I did."

All his thoughts mangled together and his heart lurched in his chest. So he kissed her again to make sure that the lightning would strike twice.

It did.

❄

Missy leaned against the front door after she closed it behind her. She ran her fingers over her lips, trying to feel the sensation of Dylan's kiss. Trying to remember every moment of it. She couldn't ever remember any kiss electrifying her like that. Charging her emotions with a whirlwind of feelings and thoughts.

Why had she never kissed Dylan before?

Becky Lee walked out of the kitchen holding a dish towel in one hand and an oven mitt in the other. "I thought I heard you come in." She paused and her brow crinkled. "You okay?"

"I am very okay." Missy pushed off the door. "I'm just fabulous."

Becky Lee laughed. "I guess the date went well?"

"We decided it was a non-date date. Best decision ever."

"You're not making much sense, Cuz."

Missy followed Becky Lee back to the kitchen where the smell of apple pie filled the air. "Well, the date started out… awkward. I thought he was having a horrible time. I couldn't get him to talk. It was… terrible."

"I thought you said it was fabulous."

"I'm getting to that." Missy sat in a kitchen chair and kicked off her shoes. "So I called him out on it. We decided to call the date a non-date, and everything went fine from then on. Better than fine."

"Fabulous. So you said." Becky Lee grinned. "So are you going out again?"

Missy sat up in alarm. "I don't know. He didn't ask me."

Just then she heard a knock at the door.

"Can you get that? I've got to get this pie out of the oven." Becky Lee turned away, barely hiding a knowing smile.

Missy went and peeked through the window of the front door. She hesitated, heart pounding, as she nervously reached for the door handle. She opened it to find a sheepish-looking Dylan.

"Dylan?"

"Hey, I forgot to ask. You want to go out again tomorrow night?"

Missy smiled. "I'd like that very much."

CHAPTER 8

Missy sat in her mother's kitchen, sipping coffee. Her mother had called first thing this morning and asked her to come over and tell her about her date with Dylan. She'd never figured out how news traveled so quickly in Comfort Crossing. Someone must have seen her and Dylan last night, who told someone, who told someone, who told her mother. That's how it usually went.

"So did you have a good time?" Her mother sat knitting at the kitchen table.

"I did."

"Well, you have been spending a lot of time with him since you got home. I'm not surprised he asked you out. He had a crush on you in high school, you know."

Missy set down her coffee cup. "Am I the only one in the whole town who didn't know that?"

Her mother smiled. "Possibly."

Missy's cell phone rang, and she pulled it from her jeans' pocket. Nashville area code, but she didn't recognize the number. "Hello?"

"Miss Sherwood? This is Keith Harper's manager. You auditioned for a backup singer a while back?"

"Yes."

"We'd like to offer you that job."

Missy sat in stunned silence. Her mother wrinkled her brow and set down her knitting.

"I. Uh, when would you need me?"

"Right away. We have a big rehearsal of his show tomorrow afternoon. Does that work for you?"

"Can I let you know?"

"I really need an answer now. We're a bit behind the eight ball now."

Missy glanced over at her mother. "Okay. I'll be there tomorrow."

Missy tapped off the phone. Her mother sat and looked at her. "And?"

"That was Keith Harper's manager. I got the backup singer job. I finally got a real life honest to goodness singing gig with a country superstar." Missy set the phone on the table and stared at it.

"Well, that's wonderful news, dear. I'm so happy for you."

"Thanks." Missy still stared at the phone.

"Did I hear you say you'd be there tomorrow? You're going to miss Christmas with us after all?"

"I guess so. I'm sorry, Mom. I know you were happy I'd finally be here for the holidays."

"Well, when opportunity knocks, you've got to answer."

She smiled at her mother. She could always depend on Mom to have a saying for every situation. Then it hit her. The Christmas play. And the nursing home Christmas party. And she'd promised to sing at Frankie's on New Year's Eve.

"What's the matter, dear? You don't look very excited."

"It's just that I made so many plans for the holidays. People depending on me..." Missy chewed her lip. "But I've waited so long to get a call like this."

"That you have." Her mother picked back up her knitting and the needles clicked through the yarn.

"What am I going to do?"

"Well, you're going to have to make that

decision for yourself. Listen to your heart. That's the only way to make a tough decision."

A sinking feeling ran through Missy. She was so torn. It's what she'd always wanted, right? What she'd planned? Yes, she'd planned for this big break her whole life. Then why did she feel so terrible?

Missy stood up from the table and looked at her mom. "I'm sorry, Mom. Please don't be disappointed. I've got to go back to Nashville."

"You're not disappointing me. You need to follow your heart. I just want you to be happy, you know that." Her mother stood up and gave her a hug. "I guess you better go pack your things."

"I do need to pack. And go by this afternoon and tell the kids I won't be here for the play. They'll be fine with Dylan leading them. They know their lines. They'll be fine."

"I'm sure they will." Her mother smiled at her encouragingly if not convincingly.

Missy stood at the door to the town hall, gathering her courage. She had a few minutes until practice was scheduled to start. She'd do this one last practice, then at the end, explain to the kids why she needed to leave. Explain to Dylan. They'd all understand. They would.

Dylan peeked his head out the door. "There you are." He came outside and took both her hands in his and pulled her to him. He looked both directions then leaned in and gave her a quick kiss. "Been wanting to do that all day. Hard to concentrate on building houses when all I could think about was another kiss." He winked at her.

She pulled back slightly and gave him a weak grin. Now was a good time to tell him. Before they went inside. He'd understand. It was her dream.

"Dylan… I need to talk to you—"

"Miss Sherwood. Miss Sherwood." Timmy came running up to the door and grabbed her hand. "Let's go in. Mom helped me with my lines. I'm better now. Come on." He tugged on her hand.

Dylan laughed. "Better go with the young man. He's got lines to say."

"But I wanted to talk to you for a minute. It's important."

"I'll catch you after practice, okay? I actually need to go run an errand for my boss. Will you be okay with the practice on your own?"

Missy nodded. Things were not going as she had planned. She'd wanted to tell him first.

"Okay, let's go in and get started." Timmy tugged on her hand again and she smiled at the boy's enthusiasm.

They went inside, she got all the kids organized, and the play opened with the children playing shopkeepers, a doctor, a vet, a teacher, and other various townsfolk. They all took their roles so seriously. The play really had come together nicely. Then it was Timmy's turn to enter the stage. He walked slowly onto the stage like she'd taught him, and then he looked furtively over at her. She nodded and mouthed his first line. He nodded back and said his opening lines without one mistake. Her heart swelled with pride. Then a wave of remorse washed over her. She was going to miss the live performance for the town. They would be fine. She was sure. But her heart ached with the knowledge she'd miss it.

After practice she had the kids gather on the stage. She cleared her throat and sucked in a deep breath. First, she needed to break the news to the kids, then she'd tell Dylan.

"I have something to tell you all." She moved up closer to the stage. "I have some news. I got called away to Nashville. I got a job with Keith Harper… do you know who he is?"

"I do." Anna stepped forward. "He's a famous country singer. My mom likes him."

"Well, the thing is… I need to go meet up with him tomorrow. My job starts tomorrow."

"In Nashville?" Timmy walked up to the front of the stage.

"Yes, in Nashville."

"But you'll miss the play. How are we going to have the play without a director?"

"You all know your parts and Dylan will still be here to direct you."

"I can't do the play if you're not here. Who will help me with my lines? You said you'd be here to help me." Timmy stood with his hands on his hips.

"Well, this job came up and I have to take it. Dylan will help you. You'll see. Everything will be fine."

Timmy looked at her, his eyes accusing and angry. "You said you'd be here." He spun on his feet, slipped his costume coat off and flung it on a chair. He climbed off the stage and rushed out the door.

The other children stood there in silence.

"You'll be great. Really. It will be fine."

The kids slowly walked away, shedding costumes and props in their wake.

She turned from the stage to see Dylan standing midway down the aisle. Her look was met with an icy stare of disbelief.

No, this wasn't going as planned. Not well at all.

Dylan turned and walked away.

"Dylan, wait," she called to him but he kept walking. She hurried after him, snatching her jacket from a chair and racing out the door.

"Dylan." She called his name again and ran to catch up to him. When she caught up, she reached and placed her hand on his elbow.

He turned to her, his eyes blazing. "You're leaving." It wasn't a question, more of a statement.

"I got the backup singer gig with Keith Harper. I have to take it. I've waited so long for a break like this."

"I see. All that talk about staying here in Comfort Crossing? You were just biding your time until something better came along?"

"That's not fair. You know it's been my dream."

"Part of your well thought out plan. The plan that I'm not part of."

"Dylan, we could still see each other…" But she knew that wouldn't really work. Not for either of them. Dylan wanted someone here, someone to share time with. Her schedule would be crazy with travel all over the states, and maybe the world.

Dylan stood silently looking at her, then bobbed his head once. "Go do what you have to do. Follow your plan. I wish you the best." He spun on his heels and walked away down Main Street.

CHAPTER 9

Missy left before daybreak to make it to Nashville for the afternoon practice. With every mile that she sped away from Comfort Crossing her spirits plummeted. Which was crazy because she was finally getting a chance to sing with a famous country singer. She should be ecstatic, crazy happy, joyful. It was all she had planned for, dreamed of.

She pulled into Nashville, realizing she needed to find a place to live now, too. Her roommates had rented her room out as soon as she left. She'd have to figure that all out now.

She walked into the soundstage and saw a crowd of singers and musicians standing around talking. She saw Keith Harper talking to his manager. She walked over to the men, squaring her shoulders, ready to start this stage of her life.

"Missy, darlin', you made it." Keith's manager reached out and shook her hand. "Keith, this is the new backup singer I was telling you about. Missy Sherwood."

Keith scrunched his face. "That name sounds familiar." He shook his head. "Anyway, nice to meet you. We can always use another backup singer." Keith flashed his well-known charming smile at her.

Not exactly what she had been expecting, but okay. What had she expected? That he'd be gushing over her and how great her voice was? Had he even heard her audition, or did someone else pick the backup singers?

The manager pointed across the room. "See that redhead over there? That's Jackie. She'll show you the ropes."

The two men turned and started talking again, oblivious to the fact she was standing there next to them feeling lost and dismissed.

She crossed the room and introduced herself to Jackie. "I'm the new backup singer. Missy."

"Hey, Missy. Heard we were getting some more backup. Why don't you sit over there?" She pointed to a chair in the corner. "You'll need to learn the music, too. I'll send it home with you tonight. For today, why don't you just listen."

Missy crossed the room and sat in the chair while the musicians and singers got ready to practice. Practice went on for hours, and she sat patiently listening. With each minute that went by her heart wobbled in her chest. She glanced at her watch and realized the kids would be practicing the play now without her. *Without her.* And just like that, she knew she had made the wrong decision. She'd been blindly following her plan. Because she always followed her plan.

But maybe, just maybe, her plan was wrong.

"Let's take a fifteen-minute break." Keith set his guitar down and crossed the room towards her.

Now was the time to tell him. Tell him she'd made a mistake.

"I finally remembered where I'd heard your name. It was on a demo of a song I really liked. It was called My Town. That was you, right?"

She stood up. "It was."

"Darn good song. Good melody, great words."

"Thank you."

He wasn't making this any easier on her, but she realized, even with his compliment on her demo, she still didn't want this life anymore. She wanted to go home.

"So is My Town about where you live?"

"It is. Comfort Crossing, Mississippi. A small town near the gulf coast. About an hour out of New Orleans."

"You got more of those songs?"

"I do."

"I'd like to hear them sometime." Keith stood there, presenting her with her dreams on a platter.

Her heart pounded so loudly she could barely hear over her pulse racing through her. "I can get you more demos if you want, but…"

Keith Harper, for goodness' sake, stood there waiting for her to finish her sentence.

"But I don't think I can take the singer job. I really need to be home for the holiday this year. People are depending on me. I just… want to be home for the holidays. Actually… I want to move back there and live. A change of plans."

Keith smiled at her. "Nothing wrong with wanting to be home for the holidays. I miss that myself. We'll find us another backup singer."

"I'm sorry for the confusion. The yes I'll take the job, no I need to leave."

"You know what? We all have to find what makes us happy in life and where we find that happiness. For me, it's here in Nashville. Sounds like for you it's back in 'My Town.'"

"Thank you for being so understanding."

Keith flashed that smile at her again. "You go have a good holiday. Tell you what though, I have a benefit concert coming up in New Orleans. I'll have my manager contact you. I'd like to get together with you and talk. I'd really like the rights to My Town and I'd like to hear some more of your work. If that small town of yours gives you your inspiration for songs like My Town, then that's probably where you should be."

"Really?" Missy had to keep from clapping her hands. "I mean, that would be great."

"Y'all have a safe trip back home and a good holiday. I'll talk to you after the new year." He shook her hand and turned to go talk to one of the singers.

Missy stood looking around the room. This is what she thought she'd wanted. To be a singer. To be part of Keith's entourage. All this is what she planned. But in the space of an afternoon, she knew her plans were all wrong for her now. She knew what she wanted, and she knew where she needed to go.

❄

Timmy sat on the bench outside of Magnolia Cafe. His mom was inside with Miss Becky Lee and Miss Jenny, her friends. She'd offered for him to come in and have a milkshake, but he needed to learn his lines for the play. He'd written each line down on notecards and slowly shuffled through them.

"Hi there, young man." An old man stood beside the bench. "What are you working on?"

"My lines for the Christmas play. I get to be the stranger this year. Before I was too little and got to be stuff like a star or an elf. I'm the main guy this year."

"That sounds like a pretty important job."

Timmy sighed. "Yeah, but I keep messing up. Miss Sherwood was gonna be there to help me, but now she's gone. I'm never gonna remember everything."

"I'll tell you what. How about I work on those lines with you? I'm Mr. Nick, by the way." The man sat down next to him.

"Hi, Mr. Nick." Timmy handed the man the cards and started reciting his first line, but he forgot the second line. Timmy jumped up. "See, I'll never get it right."

"Have you been working on it a lot?"

"Every day."

"Then, I'll tell you what. I'll let you borrow my lucky scarf."

"You have a lucky scarf?"

Timmy eyed the winter scarf Mr. Nick was wearing.

"Yep, and when someone wears it, it makes their wishes come true."

"Nah, it doesn't."

"Sure does. You got any Christmas wishes?"

"Well, I wished for a puppy, but Mom isn't too excited about that. And I wished to not mess up my lines and look like a dork."

"Tell you what. You wear this lucky scarf at the play. You'll remember all your lines."

Timmy scowled. "You sure?"

"I'm sure." Mr. Nick stood up. "Just wear it, you'll see."

Timmy stared at the scarf Mr. Nick had draped around his neck. A lucky scarf. He hadn't known there were such things as lucky scarfs. He smiled, picked up his cards, and ran through his lines without making even one mistake.

CHAPTER 10

Missy pulled into the parking lot of the Comfort Crossing nursing home, her car crammed full of all her belongings. She glanced at her watch. She was a few minutes late, but she'd made it. She hurried into the building. She saw her mother across the room, handing out presents to the residents gathered by the large Christmas tree in the lobby.

Her mother looked up and a huge smile spread across her face. She reached up a hand and touched her heart. Missy was pretty sure the look on her mother's face was all she needed for Christmas this year.

Well, that and Dylan's forgiveness. She crossed the lobby and knelt down beside Mrs. Greene's wheelchair. "Missy, my dear. How good to see you." The woman leaned forward and hugged her.

"It's great to see you, too. Merry Christmas."

Missy stood back up and walked over to her mother. "You were right, Mom. Sometimes you just need to follow your heart."

"Well, I'm glad to have you home." Her mother hugged her then laughed. "Here, help me play Santa."

Missy took a pile of packages and played Santa's helper to her mother's Santa. After the presents were opened, she sat at the piano in the lobby and sang Christmas songs with the residents. This is what Christmas was all about. The giving of time. Bringing joy to others.

They finished up their carols and Missy stood up from the piano. "Mom, I need to go. I want to get to play practice."

"Okay, you run along." Her mother reached out to stop her. "And, dear? I'm glad you figured out what you really wanted."

"Me, too, Mom. Me, too." Missy hurried out to her car, anxious to get to town hall and help with the play. And see Dylan. She needed to talk to Dylan.

❄

Missy got to town hall and rushed inside. She couldn't wait to tell the kids she'd be there for the play after all. She walked down to the front of the stage. The kids were running around getting dressed in costumes. Dylan was nowhere in sight.

Timmy's mother, Bella, came up to her. "Dylan got tied up at work. He called and asked me to stand in for him. As you can see, I have nothing under control." Bella paused and looked at her. "Timmy said that you'd left town. That you weren't going to be here for the play. He was really upset."

"I'm sorry I upset him. I needed to… well, I needed to figure some things out."

"Miss Sherwood. You're back." Timmy climbed off the stage and rushed over to wrap his arms around her waist. "You're going to stay, right?"

"I'm going to stay, Timmy. Sorry for leaving. I have it all sorted out now."

"Mom, not that you aren't a good director, but Miss Sherwood is here now, so you can go."

Bella laughed. "I think I'll take you up on the suggestion. I'm good at a lot of things, but directing the Christmas play isn't one of them. I'm going to run over to Magnolia Cafe and see

Becky Lee while you practice. You meet me there, okay?"

"Okay, Mom. I gotta practice now." Timmy climbed back up on the stage. "Come on, guys. Miss Sherwood is back. We gotta practice."

Missy knew she was back where she belonged. Where she wanted to be. Where she was needed. "Let's start from the beginning."

They ran through the play, then Missy had them sit on the stage.

"I have a surprise, but I need your help."

"We'll help you, Miss Sherwood." Anna bobbed her head.

"But we need to keep it a secret."

"I can keep a secret real good." Timmy nodded his head vigorously.

She let them in on her secret and they all agreed to help her.

CHAPTER 11

Dylan pulled up in front of town hall even though he was pretty sure he'd missed all the practice. He couldn't help it. Steve had needed him to help finish up the house they'd built because they'd promised it would be ready by tomorrow morning. He'd felt terrible asking Timmy's mom for help, but hadn't known where else to turn.

He walked into town hall and saw all the kids were already gone. Then he saw her. Missy. Standing on the stage and collecting the costumes.

"Dylan." She stood up when she saw him.

"What are you doing here?" He stood where he was, not willing to move any closer.

She jumped down from the stage and crossed the distance to him. "I came home."

"What about your plans? Your big break?"

"I decided that maybe plans change. I came home to help with the play. I just couldn't miss it."

"And then?"

"I plan on staying in Comfort Crossing." She reached her hand out towards him.

He took a step back. "But your plans change often, don't they?"

"Dylan, I'm sorry. I didn't mean to hurt you. To disappoint the kids. I just needed time to figure things out."

"I'm sure the kids appreciate that you'll be here for the play." He knew his voice sounded cold and flat. He couldn't help it. He was not going to open up his heart to this woman who kept changing her plans, dragging him along for the ride.

"The kids do seem excited. I'm so glad I came back." She stood there waiting, her eyes filled with hope.

Well, he didn't know what she expected, but all he knew was he needed to get out of here. Fast. "If you have it under control, then I'll let you manage it all tomorrow. That will probably be for the best."

"You're not even going to help?" The disappointment was clear in her voice.

"You'll be fine." She'd thought he'd be fine handling it alone, so she sure as heck could handle it alone herself. He turned to leave.

"Dylan, wait. Do you think you could give me a second chance? Could we just start over?"

"I don't think so. I'm not going to take the chance you'll change your plans yet again." With that, he walked out of the town hall on out onto Main Street. He looked up and down the street, at the bright Christmas lights, at the townspeople hurrying along with their last minute shopping. He didn't want to go back to his lonely house and sit staring at his Christmas tree.

Seeing Missy again had been a punch in the gut. He'd thought it would be years until she dropped into town again, maybe he would have been able to handle it after some time had passed. He'd thought that maybe the next time he'd see her would be on TV, singing with some star, or maybe a star herself. He sure hadn't planned on her being back here. At the play. Saying she was here to stay.

He turned the other direction and headed to Frankie's. It would be loud and bright and he could lose himself in the familiar mayhem that was Frankie's.

❄

Shawn slid into the chair across from Dylan. "What's up? The scowl on your face is scaring people away."

"Not up for joking around."

"Who's joking?" Shawn shifted in his chair. "Really. What's wrong?"

"Everything." Dylan knew that sounded overly dramatic, but it was how he felt.

"Is it because Missy left town? Belinda told me she left. I was afraid of that. Missy has her plans."

"She did leave."

"I'm sorry."

"Don't be." Dylan took a swig of his beer. "She's back."

"What?" Shawn sat up straight.

"I saw her at town hall after play practice."

"So she came back to do the play? Back for the holidays?"

"She says she's back for good." He stared into his drink, looking for answers. The beer wasn't offering up any clues.

"Well, that's good, isn't it? It seemed like you guys were getting close." Shawn cocked an eyebrow and sent him a questioning gaze.

"We were until she all of a sudden, after

swearing she was staying here, just up and left for Nashville." Dylan could still feel the hurt, deep in the pit of his stomach.

"But she picked coming back here over Nashville? That's big. Really big. She never strays far from her planned out path. Used to drive me nuts. I just couldn't see living my life with her like that. One of the many reasons I broke up with her." Shawn grinned. "That and we were totally wrong for each other. You two, on the other hand, seem great together."

"I thought you warned me to stay away from her. That she'd up and leave. Which she did."

"Don't be a fool. Don't you see? She came back. She chose you over Nashville. She chose Comfort Crossing."

"I don't think I can trust her not to change her mind again." Dylan stared into the still not answering beer.

"Your choice, buddy, but I think you're making a mistake. I think she's changed. Sometimes we finally grow up and realize what we always wanted from life… isn't really what we need from life or want anymore."

Shawn stood up and punched Dylan in the shoulder. "Think about it."

Dylan just sat and stared at his beer, still

hoping it would show him the answer like someone staring at tea leaves trying to read their fortune.

CHAPTER 12

"Timmy, where did you get that scarf?" Missy stared at the winter white cabled scarf tied around Timmy's neck.

"This old man, Mr. Nick, gave it to me to wear tonight. Said it made wishes come true. 'Cause I wished I'd remember all my lines so people won't laugh at me. He told me to wear it during the play. It's a lucky scarf."

Mr. Nick, the same man she'd met in the park. Well, if it helped give Timmy confidence, then scarf with his costume it was.

She looked out into the audience, scanning the crowd for Dylan, but she saw no sign of him. Her mother sat near the front with Dwayne and waved to her. Missy waved back then turned to the kids. "Everyone ready?"

They all nodded, their eyes wide with excitement. "Okay then. It's time to start."

The lights dimmed and the music of the first song started. The kids' faces glowed with excitement and when it was time for Timmy's entrance, he strutted on stage and glanced at her. She smiled at him and nodded, and he said his lines, loud and clear.

At the end of the play, the kids basked in their standing ovation. She was so proud of them. The whole play, and practices, and getting to know the kids had been so rewarding.

Timmy walked up to the microphone at the edge of the stage. "'Scuse, me." He tapped the mic. "Hey, we have one more special surprise this year." The audience quieted down and sat back in their seats.

Missy walked out onto the stage and sat on a stool. "This song is for someone special. Someone who showed me this town means everything to me. I'd lost my way for a lot of years, but now I'm back. I'm home."

She strummed the guitar and started into the first verse of My Town. The audience grew quiet as she sang the words of her heart. About her town, their town, Comfort Crossing. The kids joined in on the chorus, just like she'd taught them yesterday at practice.

As she finished up the last verse, and the kids' voices drifted off after the last chorus, the entire town hall was silent for a moment. A lone person stood up in the back and started clapping, breaking the silence.

Dylan.

The entire audience jumped to their feet, clapping. The applause washed over her, but all she could see was Dylan walking towards her down the center aisle.

He got to the front and swung easily onto the stage. She set her guitar down. He reached down and took her hands and pulled her to her feet.

"Missy Sherwood. I'm a fool. And one other thing. I love you. Should have said that before." He leaned down right there on stage and kissed her in front of the whole town.

"Yuck, they're kissing," Timmy piped up.

"That's 'cause they're in love," Anna said with her seven years of knowledge.

"I love you, too," Missy whispered, with no thought of the microphone placed directly in front of her, picking up every heartfelt word. The audience was once again on their feet, clapping and cheering their approval.

Dylan looked at her and grinned. "Guess it's no longer a secret." He wrapped his arms around her and held her close.

Dylan and Missy took a stroll along Main Street on Christmas Day, trying to walk off the big Christmas dinner they'd had at her mother's house. Dylan held her hand in his as they strolled. They cut through the town park and walked by the gazebo.

She looked up and saw Timmy and his brother come running towards them. "Miss Sherwood. Look what I got for Christmas." Timmy scooped up the puppy he and his brother were taking for a walk. "A puppy. I got a puppy."

She bent down to pet the pup. "He's adorable."

"His name is Nick. After that Mr. Nick guy."

"That's a great name for a puppy." Dylan petted the dog.

"Oh, and Miss Sherwood." Timmy put the dog down and took off the cabled scarf he was still wearing. "Mr. Nick said when I was done with the scarf, to give it to someone else so their wishes could come true." Timmy tugged her down so he could wrap the scarf around her neck. "Here, you get your wish now. You know, Mr. Nick was just like the stranger in the play. Granting Christmas wishes. I didn't mess up my lines and I got a puppy."

"Thank you, Timmy." Missy watched as Timmy and his brother raced back across the park. She reached up and touched the scarf. It all felt right to her now, like the last jigsaw puzzle piece had fallen into place. She'd spent so long chasing a dream, a dream she didn't even have anymore. Maybe the real dream was just finding happiness.

"So you think that scarf will make all your wishes come true?" Dylan stood before her, his eyes a reflection of the love exploding within her.

"I do." She stood up on her tiptoes and kissed Dylan.

Out of the corner of her eye, she saw a lone man standing at the edge of the park. Dylan kissed her again, and when she opened her eyes the man was gone. She slipped her hand in Dylan's.

All her wishes had come true.

I hope you enjoyed these holiday stories in the Comfort Crossing Series. Did you miss the start of the series? Book one, The Shop on Main, is available for FREE. Click here to download your free copy. The Shop on Main

Or get a good deal and a jump start on the series with the boxed set of Books 1-3 plus a short story. Comfort Crossing Boxed Set - Book 1, 2, 3.

Follow along with three lifelong friends — Bella, Jenny, and Becky Lee — as they navigate the heartaches and triumphs of love and life in the small Southern town of Comfort Crossing.

ALSO BY KAY CORRELL

THANK YOU for reading my story. I hope you enjoyed it. Sign up for my newsletter to be updated with information on new releases, promotions, give-aways, and newsletter-only surprises. The signup is at my website, kaycorrell.com.

Reviews help other readers find new books. I always appreciate when my readers take time to leave an honest review.

I love to hear from my readers. Feel free to contact me at authorcontact@kaycorrell.com

COMFORT CROSSING ~ THE SERIES

The Shop on Main - Book One

The Memory Box - Book Two

The Christmas Cottage - A Holiday Novella (Book 2.5)

The Letter - Book Three

The Christmas Scarf - A Holiday Novella (Book 3.5)

The Magnolia Cafe - Book Four

The Unexpected Wedding - Book Five

The Wedding in the Grove (crossover short story between series - Josephine and Paul from The Letter.)

LIGHTHOUSE POINT ~ THE SERIES

Wish Upon a Shell - Book One

Wedding on the Beach - Book Two

Love at the Lighthouse - Book Three

Cottage near the Point - Book Four

Return to the Island - Book Five

Bungalow by the Bay - Book Six

SWEET RIVER ~ THE SERIES

A Dream to Believe in - Book One

A Memory to Cherish - Book Two

A Song to Remember - Book Three

A Time to Forgive - Book Four

A Summer of Secrets - Book Five

A Moment in the Moonlight - Book Six

INDIGO BAY ~ Save by getting Kay's complete collection of stories previously published separately in the multi-author Indigo Bay series. The three stories are all interconnected.

Sweet Days by the Bay

Or by them separately:

Sweet Sunrise - Book Three

Sweet Holiday Memories - A short holiday story

Sweet Starlight - Book Nine

ABOUT THE AUTHOR

Kay writes sweet, heartwarming stories that are a cross between women's fiction and contemporary romance. She is known for her charming small towns, quirky townsfolk, and enduring strong friendships between the women in her books.

Kay lives in the Midwest of the U.S. and can often be found out and about with her camera, taking a myriad of photographs which she likes to incorporate into her book covers. When not lost in her writing or photography, she can be found spending time with her ever-supportive husband, knitting, or playing with her puppies—two cavaliers and one naughty but adorable Australian shepherd. Kay and her husband also love to travel. When it comes to vacation time, she is torn between a nice trip to the beach or the mountains—but the mountains only get considered in the summer—she swears she's allergic to snow.

Learn more about Kay and her books at kaycorrell.com

While you're there, sign up for her newsletter to hear about new releases, sales, and giveaways.

WHERE TO FIND ME:

kaycorrell.com
authorcontact@kaycorrell.com

Join my Facebook Reader Group. We have lots of fun and you'll hear about sales and new releases first!
https://www.facebook.com/groups/KayCorrell/

facebook.com/KayCorrellAuthor
instagram.com/kaycorrell
pinterest.com/kaycorrellauthor
amazon.com/author/kaycorrell
bookbub.com/authors/kay-correll

Made in the USA
Middletown, DE
26 November 2022